POPULATION ZERO

WRATH JAMES WHITE

deadite
press

deadite press

DEADITE PRESS
205 NE BRYANT
PORTLAND, OR 97211
www.DEADITEPRESS.com

AN ERASERHEAD PRESS COMPANY
www.ERASERHEADPRESS.com

ISBN: 1-936383-37-3

"Population Zero" first appeared as a limited edition hardback by Cargo Cult Press, 2009.

Printed in the USA.

Prologue

Honey's stomach undulated beneath Todd's hand as he rubbed her bloated belly. He could see the faint impressions of little faces and tiny paws stretching her flesh as the puppies moved around inside of her. The golden retriever had crawled back into the far corner of the closet, panting heavily, struggling to give birth. Blood and fluid dripped from her vagina while she paced around the tiny closet in a tight circle, squatting occasionally as if she were trying to defecate. Her body quivered and her legs shook from the exertion.

"Come on, Honey. You're doing fine, girl."

He filled her water bowl and Honey lapped feverishly at the water.

"That's a good girl."

Todd stroked her fur while she continued to drink.

He was excited. Honey was his best friend. She had been his since he was just a year old. Todd could not remember a time when she hadn't been by his side. She was, for the most part, his only friend. His mother was deeply religious and had home schooled him rather than send him to public school, saving him from a "heathenous secular education."

"It's no wonder there's all these kids out there shooting each other, using drugs, alcohol, and smoking cigarettes now that they've taken the Bible out of school. They won't even let the kids pray! Then they teach them sex education and wonder why they're all having under-aged premarital sex and making babies out of wedlock. There's no way I'd let my baby go to one of those godless schools. Everything you need to know is right here in the Bible."

He wasn't allowed to play with any of the neighborhood kids, who his mother regarded as sinners, deviants, and criminals. So, Honey had been his only playmate. She slept at the foot of his bed, to his mother's chagrin, but the one time his mother had locked the dog out of Todd's room he'd cried himself hoarse. His mother had finally relented and Honey had been sleeping with him ever since. When she had gotten pregnant he'd been so excited. Puppies would mean even more friends to help cure his agonizing loneliness.

Honey began licking herself and then lay down on her side. The first puppy slid out still encased in a sack of amniotic fluid. Honey licked and nibbled at the sack as she pushed out the next small sack. She ate the membrane off of each puppy, as she continued to push them out—chewing them free and then licking them clean. Todd was so happy, he was in tears.

"They're beautiful, Honey. Look at all of your babies. You did it, girl."

He reached out and rubbed the dog's head as Honey lay back down, still panting from exhaustion.

"Ah, Jesus! Look at that mess in there!"

Todd's dad stood behind him, still wearing his muddy work boots and his grey Dickies shirt with the sweat stains in the armpits.

"Mom says you shouldn't take the lord's name in vain. I'll clean it up, Dad. Aren't they pretty though? I watched the whole thing. You should have seen it. It was amazing!"

"Yeah? How many of them are there?"

Todd looked back over at Honey, who was still cleaning her puppies.

"Eleven."

"Eleven? Jesus, we can't afford to feed eleven puppies. We can barely afford Honey."

"But, Dad, we can't sell 'em!"

"You'd better hope we can sell 'em or else they're going to the animal shelter."

Todd began to cry.

"No. No, Dad. You can't. No."

"Come here, son."

Todd walked over to his father who knelt down beside him.

"Look, son, I know you want to keep them but we can't

4

afford to feed them."

"But on T.V. they said they kill puppies at the animal shelters. They put 'em to sleep."

"Well, if they didn't there'd be dogs and cats everywhere. We'd be drowning in 'em. They'd eat up all of the food and they'd be dying in the streets of starvation and disease. Putting them to sleep is the humane thing to do. It keeps 'em from suffering. In the wild they had predators that helped keep their population down but since we took 'em out of the wild there's nothing to keep 'em from just continuing to reproduce. There's no wolves or lions or anything to compete with for food or kill off the old, the sick and the weak ones."

"Well, what about us?"

"That's what I'm talking about. We help keep their numbers down painlessly and humanely by putting them to sleep when people can't take care of them."

Todd looked back over at Honey. The puppies were now blindly reaching for her nipples, trying to suckle. Honey nudged them gently with her nose to help them find her teats. They looked so weak and helpless. Todd couldn't imagine them being sent to the pound and murdered. He began to sob. His father reached out and hugged him close. Todd knew that his father loved him even if he didn't always understand him. "I know. It's hard. But it's the right thing. We just can't afford to feed them all. Either we eat or they do."

"But what about us? We don't have any predators either. What happens when there are too many people?"

"Well, we have diseases and wars and disasters."

"But we keep curing all the diseases."

"There's a whole bunch that we haven't cured."

"The newsman said that there's like six billion people alive right now. Only a hundred thousand people died in the Gulf War."

"A hundred thousand is a lot of people."

"Not compared to six billion."

"Well, there 're more wars than that going on. There are wars going on all over the place."

"That's still not enough. If we have to kill Honey's puppies to keep there from being too many dogs then why aren't we doing the same with people?"

"Todd!"

Todd stared up at his father. He could see the man's frustration as he rubbed a coarse calloused hand over his furrowed brow. He was visibly exhausted. His father let out a sigh and reached down to wipe a tear from Todd's eyes. Todd knew that he was just speaking out of anger and frustration but it just didn't make sense to him. Todd stared back at his father, waiting for an answer, waiting for his father to make it all make sense. Waiting for his father to explain why it was okay to put his puppies to sleep because there were too many of them while humans were still multiplying like roaches. Past the tears still welling in his son's eyes, Todd's father could see the anger boiling there. He didn't know what to do about it.

"Son, you shouldn't talk like that. What would your Mom say if she heard you talkin' about billions of people dyin'? That's not very Christian."

"But what's going to happen, Daddy? What's going to happen when there's no more room? What happens when there's not enough food for everybody?"

"I don't know, baby. I'm not sure. But that's probably not something we need to worry about in our lifetime. Maybe that's when the rapture your Momma's always talkin' about will come or maybe we'll all get in a big spaceship and go to another planet."

Todd looked past his father, across the room, and out his bedroom window. The stars were out. They looked so far away. He couldn't imagine everyone on the planet getting in one spaceship and making it so far. It just didn't seem possible. If Jesus didn't come down and get them all, Todd was fairly certain that everyone in the world would look like those pictures of starving children he saw on television once the population inevitably doubled. He looked back over at Honey. One of the puppies was smaller than all the rest. The other puppies weren't letting him in to feed.

"Can I keep the little one?"

"We'll see."

A month later they sold three of the puppies. Two weeks after that, they took the other eight to the animal shelter. Todd cried for a week.

One

Todd could not understand how some of these people had the nerve to come into his cubicle, begging for welfare and food stamps, claiming that they couldn't afford to buy food on their own, when they were clearly 50 or 60 or even 100 pounds overweight. It took a lack of humility that he simply did not possess. He watched the corpulent woman, a cascade of chins hanging down her neck and disappearing somewhere under her T-shirt. Breasts twice the size of his own head bobbling about under her shirt in a bra that was unequal to the task of containing them. Her titanic arms jiggled even more than her mammoth tits as she filled out the paperwork. Her litter of unwashed, unruly children ran around his office, fighting and whining. Todd's stomach churned. She was morbidly obese. At least a hundred pounds over what even the most liberal physician would consider a healthy weight. Her body fat percentage had to have been in the high eighties. Todd imagined that, at 5'6" tall, her entire skeletal and muscular system, organs and all, probably weighed no more than a hundred pounds, yet she was well over 250 or 260 pounds, maybe even more. That meant that there were at least 150 pounds of fat on her body.

There had to be a foot between her muscle and her skin. Just thinking about it was beginning to make Todd ill.

When she walked into his work-area it had taken a Herculean effort just for her to cross the floor. Coming to the Welfare Department was probably the most exercise she had gotten all month. Her breathing was labored from the weight of the fat on her chest. Todd could scarcely imagine what agony her heart was going through, trying to force

7

blood through those clogged arteries and capillaries. The heavy rattling wheeze coming out of her suffocating lungs made Todd terrified that she would die right there in the chair and everyone would expect him to perform CPR on her. He didn't think he had it in him. He imagined himself staring down at her as she slowly turned blue, her kids wailing and crying, begging him to help, his coworkers rushing into his cubicle to see what the commotion was about and finding him just standing there doing nothing, their accusatory glares as one of them clamped their mouth onto her pie-hole to breathe life into her overburdened lungs and the other fished in between those impossibly big flabby tits for a rib cage and began chest compressions which would only make those big fat sweaty breasts jiggle more while Todd secretly hoped that she wouldn't recover. Todd was still immersed in his fantasy, his facial expression no doubt betraying his revulsion, when she said something that almost made him walk out of the office.

"I'm going to need to get on that Women and Children's program. I'm pregnant again."

"Excuse me?"

He must have heard her wrong, Todd thought. Surely she was not stupid enough to be having more kids when she couldn't feed and clothe the four unfortunate heathens she had already given birth to? Whatever happened to birth control? Who the hell keeps fucking this obese monstrosity of a woman? If she can't afford to feed herself why the hell does she keep having kids?

"I'm pregnant. I need an application for WIC."

"Why don't you have an abortion? We would be happy to pay for it."

The woman's jaw dropped.

Todd could not believe he had just said that. It had just slipped out. The job had gotten to him. Now she would tell his bosses and he would either get suspended or fired. *Unless I can convince her to do it. I'm probably going to get my ass fired anyway so why not try to do some good in my last few minutes of employment?*

The woman was still staring at him wide-eyed with her expression slowly changing from shock to outrage. He had to say something. Todd leaned over his desk and spoke to her in a conspiratorial whisper.

"Look, if you abort that baby and don't bring another kid that you can't afford into the world for the taxpayers to support then I'll see that the entire procedure is covered by the state and if you go ahead and get your tubes tied at the same time, I'll personally see to it that you never have to come into this office again. No more job hunting, no more interviews, no more paperwork. You will get your food stamps and your check every month and you'll never have to see my face again."

The woman's mouth opened and then she paused. She paused!

She was considering it. She looked down at the mewling infant in her lap with his face stained with baby food and juice, the two-year-old in the stroller beside her reeked from a diaper that needed to be changed an hour ago, the four and five-year-olds still fought over a toy one of them had stolen from the grocery store, and a look of exhaustion and resignation began to take over her face. Tears welled up in her eyes. She looked helpless and confused. Todd was surprised that he wasn't touched by it at all. For some reason, the plight of a single human never seemed to have the power to move him, not when there were 50,000 species of plant and animal life going extinct every year as we cleared rainforests and turned them into cattle farms so that fat whores like this could get cheeseburgers. He wanted to look away but he knew that he had to look sympathetic if he wanted to save his job.

"What do I have to sign?"

"I'll get you a medical hardship form. I'll fill out everything. You just sign the bottom of it. You are doing the right thing."

It took a supreme effort for him to keep the smile off of his face.

He looked at the long line standing outside the door of his cubicle and for the first time he didn't feel the usual anxiety. He didn't feel the desire to hide under the desk or flee the building or take an AR15 rifle and mow down everyone in sight and then burn the place to the ground.

For the first time in his nine years working for the Welfare Department, Todd Hammerstein actually felt like he had done some good.

Two

It had taken a great deal of restraint for Todd not to extend his offer of sterilization in exchange for free government money to every man or woman who walked through the door that day. He knew that he ought to be cautious. But as he watched a woman stagger in, obviously wired on methamphetamines, carrying a screaming newborn that had probably been born addicted to meth—tried to imagine what the first 24 hours of that baby's life had been like in an incubator withdrawing from drugs and what his future no doubt held—Todd could hardly hold himself back.

What was wrong with our society that we allowed this type of trash to reproduce?

One after another they came in. A man who had just gotten paroled a month ago, had ten kids by six different women spread out all over town, and was clearly avoiding paying child support by not working. A couple who were third generation welfare recipients and already had two kids, now shamelessly discussing the possibility of giving birth to another in order to get more welfare money. A single mom whose mother raised her three kids while she hopped from nightclub to nightclub. And a single dad trying to get on disability that had quit one job after another, claiming everything from Lupus to Chronic Fatigue Syndrome to Attention Deficit Disorder.

Todd wanted to sterilize them all. He wished that he didn't even have to ask. He thought that there should have been a button he could push that would call orderlies to strap them down in their chairs while he spayed and neutered them like cats.

He wondered if any of them would have taken his offer. He thought he'd better not try to find out. He had gotten lucky with the fat woman. It was best not to push his luck.

Todd went through all of the usual motions, setting them up with job interviews that he knew they wouldn't attend, recommending trade schools that they showed even less interest in, giving them pamphlets on safe sex and drug rehab programs while they sat there looking bored and impatient, waiting to fill out the paperwork so they could get their check next month. His success earlier in the day with the fat woman was beginning to recede from memory. Sure there were many more honest hardworking couples who had been laid off because of the recession or had seen their mortgage payments double because of adjustable rate interest-only loans or had otherwise fallen on hard times. They were the ones who would be off of welfare in a year. But 40% of the people who came to his office would never find jobs. Three quarters of the remaining 60% would find jobs only to lose them again in an endless pattern that would see them in and out of his office year after year. By the time the last client of the day entered his cubicle, Todd was unable to control himself. He just hoped that he would be as lucky with them as he had been with the fat woman.

"Come in. Sit down."

He looked them over, reading their entire history in their nervous jittery motions and disheveled appearance before he'd even opened their file.

They were both crack addicts, both prostitutes, expecting their first child. Sometimes it seemed as if every welfare recipient that came into his office was either pregnant or carrying a newborn. The less educated they were, the more fucked up their lives were, the more prone they appeared to be to reproduce. That alone convinced Todd that he was doing the right thing.

"How far along are you?"

The woman squinted. Her eyes rolled slowly to the left, passing by him without seeing him at all as if she were looking for something in the dark. She brushed her oily unwashed blonde hair away from her face, revealing a face dotted with a profusion of pockmarks and scabs, some of them bleeding from where she had nervously picked at them. Her eyes rolled back to the right, overshot him again and then rolled back the opposite direction before finally fixing on Todd's face. She smiled, displaying teeth blackened with cavities and the pus-filled craters where teeth had long ago rotted away or been knocked out by some angry trick. She licked her chapped lips and scratched the bleeding scabs along her arms.

"W-What?"

"Bitch, he asked you how many months pregnant you are."

The man who'd walked in with her, whom Todd assumed was her husband, grabbed the woman's arm and shook her. Her eyes focused for a second and she smiled awkwardly. The man rolled his eyes and sneered. A drop of saliva drooled from the corner of the woman's mouth and she wiped it away with the back of her hand, and then used the same hand to wipe her nose.

"Oh, I'm five months."

She smiled again and her eyes swam in her skull as if she had once again lost sight of him. Todd caught a whiff of her breath as she handed their welfare application across the desk to Todd. He wrinkled his nose. It smelled like raw sewage. She was wearing a halter top with no bra. Her breasts were small and sagged as if deflated. The nipples poked at the fabric of her halter top. Her naked stomach bulged out over the top of her miniskirt which had slipped down on her hips so far that her pubic hair was visible. She had a butterfly tattoo on her belly and a pierced navel. A dark black tribal tattoo spiraled up her skinny calves.

"What drugs are you on?"

"Man, fuck you! We ain't no drug addicts! We ain't got to answer shit for you."

Todd looked the woman's husband over. His eyes were bloodshot and weepy. He was scratching himself and jittering just as she was. Only, instead of the gap-toothed smile his wife wore, his face was twisted into a disdainful sneer. His wrinkled t-shirt was stained with blood and what looked like vomit and was at least two sizes too large as were his baggy jeans that sagged off of his bony hips. His hair was dyed black and stood up in a spiky tangle off the top of his head. He had a teardrop tattoo in the corner of his left eye and a piercing in his right eyebrow along with one in his lip. A Metallica tattoo wrapped around his neck in two inches letters, and a dragon tattoo wound up his right arm, disappearing under the sleeve of his t-shirt.

Todd smiled.

"If you want a dime of government money you'll sit down, shut the fuck up, and answer whatever questions I ask you."

"Fuck that shit! You can't talk to us like that."

"Baby! We need this money. Just come sit down."

Todd smiled warmly.

"So, what are you on?"

"Um…well…we both use crack and meth and sometimes heroin when we can get it."

Todd looked over at her husband, who looked away from him.

"Yeah, what she said and…and I use dust, I mean, PCP, sometimes too."

"What are your names?"

"My name's Nicolene De Marco and this is my husband Michael."

"How old are you two?"

"I'm 22 and Michael's 25. We're trying to get on welfare. We're expecting our second child."

"What happened to the first one?"

"He was born with some mental handicaps and a bad heart. We couldn't afford to take care of a sick baby so we had to give him up for adoption."

"And now you're having another one?"

"Yeah, but don't worry. We're both going to kick before the baby's born. Michael's going to get a job as soon as he's well. We're going to be good parents."

Todd shook his head.

"No. You won't be good parents and you're not going to get sober."

"Fuck you, man! You don't know shit about us!"

Todd leaned forward and stared directly into the eyes of the young drug addict.

"Do you really believe that? Do you really think that I haven't heard your story a hundred times before? I even know what you apparently don't, how this story ends. Care to hear it? You'll get your welfare check if I'm dumb enough to give it to you. You'll shoot it all into your arm or up your nose until you finally miscarry or else give birth to another kid with birth defects because his mom didn't give enough of a fuck about him

13

to stay off of drugs for even nine months. You'll give this kid up for adoption too because deep down you know what shitty parents you would be. And if by some miracle your kid comes out with nothing more serious than a bad case of withdrawal, you'll take it back to whatever hovel you're living in right now and feed him and change his diapers only when you're sober enough to remember. If he survives repeated infections from bad diaper rashes, malnourishment, neglect, and the physical abuse you'll no doubt subject him to when his crying blows your high, that in itself would be a miracle. But then you'd eventually lose your apartment or get kicked out of whoever's house you're crashing at and since the government can't give you a check without an address to send it to you'll wind up right back on the streets where you'll both go back to selling your ass for a hit of crack. Then one day some pedophile will offer you money for a few hours with your kid and you'll sell his ass too."

Nicolene's eyes widened. Her bottom lip trembled and she began to cry.

"I-I wouldn't…I'd never do that to my baby." Her eyes were still rolling around in her head, still unable to focus. Her brow furrowed as she tried to sober up through sheer force of will. She was obviously having trouble thinking clearly.

"Yes, you would. You'd do all of that and more. That's why the world would be better off, your baby would be better off, if you'd just have an abortion and get yourself fixed so that you can never get pregnant again. Then you can go back to smoking crack and shooting smack until you kill yourselves."

Nicolene stared across the desk at Todd, her mouth hanging open. She looked as if she were still waiting for the punch line, trying to decide if the tall, skinny redheaded white guy in the yellow polo shirt and khaki pants was really serious. Todd's smile never left his face but Nicolene could tell by the look in his eyes that he was completely serious. She was used to tough love. She'd had her fair share of family interventions over the years. But no one had ever spoken to her with this type of brutal, sadistic honesty.

She hugged herself and began to rock back and forth in the seat. Her husband looked wild-eyed from his wife to Todd. His pulse rate was jacking up. He looked like he was about to explode. Todd was expecting the man to jump up and punch

14

him right in the jaw at any second. The guy was just as skinny as he was but Todd was skinny because he ran every day, rode a bicycle to work, and didn't eat meat or dairy products. This guy was skinny because he hardly ate at all and was constantly jacked up on amphetamines. If he was on PCP he might have been able to pull Todd's arms off like the wings of a fly if he got mad enough.

"But," Nicolene looked over at her husband who was staring back at her blankly, his face betraying his shock and confusion, the rage still boiling there just under the surface, "we don't believe in abortion."

Todd rolled his eyes and shook his head in exasperation. "Obviously you don't believe in birth control either. Look at yourselves. Do you really think you'd be any good to a kid? Do you want your kid's life to be even more fucked up than yours?"

Michael sprang from his chair and jabbed his finger into Todd's face. Todd winced and prepared for a blow.

"You son-of-a-bitch! We don't have to listen to this shit! Who the fuck do you think you are?"

"No. You absolutely do not. You can walk right out that door if you'd like. I'll just stamp rejected on your welfare application and you can go back to turning tricks for drug money."

Michael sighed and slumped down in his chair.

"You know damn well we can't do that shit. We're sick, man! We need some cash."

"Well, even if I approve you now, the most you could get today would be food stamps. You wouldn't see a check for another month."

"A month!"

"Six to eight weeks actually."

"Shit! This is a waste of fucking time!" Michael began to pace the floor, looking lost and desperate.

"That's okay, baby. We can always sell the food stamps until the check comes."

"That's if I approve you and why should I? Like I said, I already know how this story is going to end for you and your baby."

"But—But we need it. We really need this money!"

"What if we did like you said? I mean, what if we got rid of the baby? If Nicolene had an abortion?"

15

"No. No. I can't. I won't!"

"Do you really still want to be out there two or three months from now, trying to turn tricks when you're seven or eight months pregnant? Come on, you know we ain't never gonna kick. You've probably already fucked that kid up with all the horse you've been shootin' in your arm."

"She'd have to get her tubes tied as well."

"Yeah, what if we did all of that?"

"If you had an abortion and a tubal ligation then I'd sign all the papers to make sure you got your monthly check. I'll even put a rush on it, put you down as an emergency hardship case so you can get your check sooner and I might even make a clerical error and put the son you gave up for adoption down as a dependent to get you some more money."

"But, I don't want to have an abortion."

Michael took Nicolene's track-marked arm in his hands and tried his best approximation of a sympathetic look.

"Nicky, we have to do this. You know we wouldn't be good parents anyway. Look at us. We can't bring a child into the world like this. This guy is right. This is the best thing for us to do."

"I'll go get the papers."

Todd watched as they filled out the paperwork. He reached into his safe and pulled out a book of $100 in food stamps.

"You'll get the rest in the mail, after you come in here and show me that it's been taken care of. Here's the number of a clinic that will do it all for free."

Michael and Nicolene De Marco walked out of Todd's cubicle holding hands.

For the second time that day, Todd felt as if he had truly made a difference, not just in the life of the unborn baby or that fucked up couple or that fat woman and her kids, but in the world.

Todd left that day feeling like he should skip down the sidewalk. He walked out of the building and into the parking lot with a smile chiseled into his face.

Three

Todd pedaled his ten-speed the six miles to his apartment, stopping at the mailbox on his way into the gated courtyard. He tucked the stack of bills under his arm and then tossed the supermarket fliers, dry cleaning coupons, and fast food menus into the trash can. His two favorite magazines had arrived. Vegan Times and Imperiled Planet. Todd thumbed through the magazines as he walked to his apartment. There was an article on the detoxification and weight loss benefits of raw foods, an article about famous celebrities who ate macrobiotically, and a recipe for vegan pasta made from shredded zucchini. Todd closed the magazine and opened the other one as he fished in his front pocket for his keys.

All of the positive feelings Todd had about what he had accomplished at work that day dissipated in a flash as he scanned through an article titled Zero Population. It was written by Heimlich Anattoli, the head of the environmental activist group that Todd belonged to and it was all about the group and his book of the same name. Todd had read the book last year after it had hit the bestseller's list. The statistics that Heimlich quoted on overpopulation were terrifying and humbling. The kind that makes you feel helpless and doomed, that make all of your efforts feel insignificant. The population was increasing by 76 million people a year, 2,500 every twenty minutes. At that rate of growth, even accounting for a continual increase in the death rate, the world population would hit ten billion within 50 years. That many people would completely overwhelm the earth, drain it dry of all of its natural resources and leave it a dead husk. Something had to be done.

Earlier that year he'd watched a documentary on Charles Manson in which Manson had stated that he needed to kill about two million people in order to save the planet. Two million people would hardly be a drop in the bucket in terms of overpopulation and the two unwanted children whose births he had prevented would not make a difference at all. He needed to do more. He had to find a way to convince more people.

Todd finally pulled his keys out and opened his front door. He dropped his magazines onto the coffee table and walked into his bedroom. Todd plopped down onto his bed and opened up his laptop. He went to the Zero Population message board. There was a new message from Heimlich. It was almost as if the man had read his mind.

"I know that many of you are concerned that the task is too big. You think that your efforts are too small to be significant. That there's not much one individual can do to impact an entire planet. Well, let me tell you a story.

A boy and his grandfather are walking along the beach. There are starfish all along the beach that were stranded there when the tide rolled out. The boy reaches down and picks up a starfish as they pass it and tosses it back into the ocean. He does this over and over again as they pass each starfish.

His grandfather asks him, "Why do you keep picking up those starfish?"

The boy looks up at his grandfather and answers, "Because they will die if I don't put them back in the water."

The boy's grandfather looks down the beach and then back at his grandson.

"There's dozens of miles of beach. What you're doing won't make much of a difference." The boy looks down at the starfish in his hand and then tosses it into the water.

"It will to this one."

So before you tell yourself that your efforts couldn't possibly make a difference, I want you to consider that the average human being is responsible for the deaths of 90 to 100 animals a year for food, clothing, and other consumable products and the destruction of more than an acre of trees. That's all just from one person."

Todd smiled and leaned back on his bed. It was exactly what he needed to hear.

Zero Population was an environmental group that advocated saving the planet through voluntary sterilization. Todd had had a recent vasectomy himself and had persuaded one of his co-workers to do the same. What he had done today though, was taking it to a whole different level. He had done more than convince someone to not have children. He had convinced those women to kill the babies already inside them. He wished that he could talk to Heimlich. He wanted to see if the man would approve of what he had done. He needed that support. He needed him to condone his actions.

Todd sat up in bed and pulled the laptop toward him. He scrolled down to the bottom of the message board and hit "New Thread." He took a moment to think of exactly what to say, sighed deeply, backed away from the laptop, sighed again then pulled the keyboard towards him and began to type.

What if you are already pregnant? Would you recommend that a woman have an abortion rather than bring another human into the world?

Todd's finger hovered over the keyboard as he tried to decide whether or not to hit enter. He could not stand the idea that Heimlich might not agree with what he had done. Heimlich was one of his heroes. He had read both of the man's books, The Human Plague and the bestseller that had gotten him on the front page of Millennium Magazine, the one from which the message board derived its name, Zero Population. Todd had read The Human Plague when he was in junior college and it had been like a revelation to him. It detailed the rapid expansion of the human population over the last two hundred years and its impact on the planet, from pollution and greenhouse gases to deforestation and the extinction of hundreds of thousands of plant and animal life. But it was Zero Population that had the greatest impact on Todd.

This was the book that offered Heimlich's prescription for solving the problem of overpopulation. Heimlich wanted to go one step further than China. Rather than limit every couple to one child, he believed that 90% of the world's men and women should be chemically sterilized, meat consumption limited to once per week by law, and the internal combustion engine banned. It was a radical stance and the Republican

Right had pounced on him. It wasn't long before Heimlich was on every talk show in the country defending his opinions against government sponsored environmental experts, right-wing politicians, and shock jocks. Heimlich's position had never wavered despite being ridiculed and maligned. Todd had been impressed. He'd looked him up on the internet and tried to contact him. That's how he had discovered his website and the message board. Today, however, was the first time in over a year that he had come out of lurking to post on the board. In minutes, he got his reply.

There were already eight other replies split right down the middle between people who thought that telling a woman to abort her baby would be taking it too far and would further alienate them from the other environmental groups, to those who were adamant that any woman that would bring another child into this world was a traitor to the planet. Todd scrolled all the way down the thread until he reached Heimlich's reply:

Who knows which child will be the one that finally breaks the camel's back? There is no way of telling how many people this world can accommodate before it gets completely overwhelmed and dies. That child in that woman's belly could be the one that dooms us all. Each human born is another consumer, another drain on the world's resources. If that woman can be persuaded to terminate her pregnancy then that can only help the cause. Who cares about those other environmental groups? This isn't a popularity contest. This is about the future of our planet.

Todd nodded his head in agreement. He'd gotten his answer.

Four

Todd was twelve-years-old when his mother had gotten pregnant. It was just one year after his father had taken the puppies to the pound. Todd's mother was doing that awkward squat that pregnant woman do as she lowered herself down onto the couch cushions. Her stomach was the size of a beach ball. Todd couldn't imagine why he hadn't noticed it before. Had she been hiding it? He didn't think his father had noticed either. Raymond Hammerstein worked all day at UPS driving a forklift and then at night as a security guard at the Supermarket. Todd couldn't even remember the last time he'd seen both his mother and father together in the same room.

The idea of a new brother or sister excited Todd. It meant a possible end to his loneliness. Todd jumped off the bed with a smile bursting onto his face as he pointed at her bulbous stomach. Now, Todd often wondered what his life would have been like if he hadn't noticed.

"Momma! You're pregnant!"

Todd could tell by the way she looked at him that he had said something wrong. Maybe she wasn't pregnant. Maybe she had just gained weight and he had somehow insulted her.

"Go to your room, Toddy."

Todd wondered what would have happened if he had stayed, if he hadn't turned quietly and stalked off to his room feeling sorry for himself. Maybe his mother would still be alive.

More than an hour had gone by before Honey had begun barking. Honey never barked. A shock collar had long

21

ago eliminated her urge to express herself. So her sudden outburst had shaken Todd. He knew something bad was happening and he knew that it probably involved his mom. That sad angry look in her eyes when Todd had noticed her swelling belly had warned him that something terrible was on the way. He only hoped that she wasn't going to hurt his dog. He didn't care if she hurt him. He was used to it.

Todd dropped his Wolverine comic back in the shoebox where he kept it hidden and slid it back into his closet. His mother didn't like him to read comics. She thought they were too violent. Todd had always thought it ironic that the same woman who frequently beat him with extension cords and wire hangers found the pretend violence in comic books to be too disturbing. But, to her, it was the same as pornography.

Honey was still barking when Todd stepped out into the hallway.

She was crouched outside the open bathroom door. The fur on her back was standing up and she was backing away. From inside the bathroom Todd could hear his mother moaning in pain. The hair on his neck and arms rose. Todd had a feeling that something worse than anything he could imagine was happening in the bathroom.

"Momma?"

Todd shuffled forward slowly. "Uhhhhnnn! Uh. Uh. Oh God."

"Momma? Are you okay?"

He could hear her rapid breathing. She was panting the way Honey had the night she'd given birth to her litter of puppies. Todd rushed forward, thinking maybe his mother was having the baby. He turned the corner into the bathroom, skidded on a pool of blood and fell flat on his butt. He looked up at his mother, who was squatting on the toilet with a bloody hanger still shoved up inside of her and blood pouring out of her in what looked like an endless river. It had overflown the toilet and was pouring out onto the floor in a tide of blackish red. His mother was still tugging on the hanger, making little grunting noises as she yanked at it, shoved it back up inside of herself, then yanked at it again. Her labia had been completely mangled by her efforts. Todd had never seen so much blood. He knew what his mother was doing even before he saw the tiny skull plop out of her bleeding vagina. The wire hanger had pierced the fetus's eye socket and had gone straight through its skull, which had been nearly disconnected from its body. There were gouges, big chunks of flesh completely torn away, all over its face and head from his mother's previous attempts to anchor the hanger into something in order to drag the fetus out of her. Todd screamed. His mother continued to yank on the hanger.

By the time Todd's father came home his mother had bled out. Todd sat leaning up against the blood-filled toilet in a pool of his mother's blood, cradling her in his arms, crying hysterically. She was naked with her legs spread wide, the tiny fetus spilling out of her vagina. The fetus was still attached by the umbilical cord and the coat hanger pierced its little skull.

"Oh my God! Rachael! Oh my God! What did you do? What did you do?"

Todd looked up at his father and shook his head. He opened his mouth but no words would come out. His dad kneeled down beside him. His father's eyes were wide as he looked over his dead wife.

"She-she was pregnant? Oh my God. She was pregnant! Why would she do this? Why would she do this?"

They sat like that, both kneeling in his mother's blood for what seemed like forever before his father rose and took Todd's arm, pulling him away from his dead mother. He took him into the kitchen and stripped his bloody clothes off of him then cleaned the blood from his skin with a wash rag.

"Don't worry, Toddy. Mommy is in heaven now," his father said through tears. He paused and bit down on his own hand to keep himself from sobbing hysterically then picked up the washcloth again and continued to scrub the blood from Todd's skin. "She's in heaven now. It's okay."

But Todd wasn't sure she was in heaven. He'd heard that you didn't go to heaven when you committed suicide. But he wasn't certain that she had been trying to kill herself. She was definitely trying to kill the baby though. Todd thought about the baby that had been inside of her. He was pretty sure that God would have considered what she had done murder unless maybe she'd had a really good reason.

"Was it like the puppies?"

His dad stopped scrubbing and looked up at him. Tears, a with a look of confusion and disgust, were in his father's eyes.

"What?"

"What Momma did? Was it like the puppies? Did she kill the baby because we couldn't afford it, because there would have been too many of us?"

His father shook his head and began to cry harder. He hugged Todd closely as his tears overtook him.

"I don't know, Toddy. I don't know."

Todd was led back to his room, a glass of milk and two chocolate chip cookies were placed by his bedside.

"I have to go clean up mommy now. You try to get some sleep." Todd couldn't sleep. He sat up and listened to the police and the paramedics traipsing through his home. He heard his grandparents come. Heard their desperate tears. Then he heard sounds that he would never forget, wet sticky sounds as his mother's body was moved. The worst of it was what he heard his father say to his grandfather as they stood in the hallway just outside of Todd's room.

"I don't know why she would do this. Rachael was against abortion." It was his grandfather's voice.

"The baby wasn't mine. I didn't even know she was pregnant. I've just been working so hard. I-I don't know how I didn't notice. She had to be at least eight months. I was just always so tired when I came home."

"What do you mean it wasn't yours?"

"Rachael and I had decided not to have any more children. Two years ago, I had a vasectomy. I think it was somebody at the church. I think she must have had an affair."

"That can't be."

"I would have forgiven her. I would have. She didn't have to…"

"Are you sure?"

"I'm sure. I'm sterile."

There was a pause and Todd's bedroom door opened. The two men peeked into Todd's room to make sure he was still asleep. Todd held the covers up over his face and didn't move. He didn't move again until he sure that he and his father had been left alone.

Five

Todd looked forward to going to work now. He was on a mission. A one-man mission to stop the spread of humanity one child at a time. The second day was not nearly as successful as the day before had been.

A black lady with two kids, one a teenager and one a toddler, came in. Her name was Sandra Watson. She was tall and beautiful and unmarried and pregnant. Her skin was a light coffee color, cappuccino, and her eyes were green. Her hair was long and braided in cornrows. Todd looked at her application. She was 31-years-old. She must have been about 15 when she'd had her first child.

Ms. Watson's unemployment had run out and she'd started working for a temp agency. Then she'd gotten pregnant. She was looking for welfare, food stamps, and WIC, while she went to nursing school.

"That's great that you're in nursing school. It must be hard being pregnant and already being a mom and still working part-time."

"Yeah, it's difficult. But Jamal helps out. I work for a temp agency during the day and my sister watches the babies. She works at night. Then Jamal babysits for me after school so I can go to school."

"You're lucky then."

"Yeah, he's the man of the house now."

Todd looked over at the shy young kid. He had a caramel complexion with a mixture of African and Caucasian features. Thick lips but a thin nose. Hazel eyes and high cheekbones. He had obviously inherited his mother's good looks. His hair was cut short, almost to the skin. He wore a baggy T-shirt and name brand jeans that hung off of his hips. Both looked new. He had a silver chain around his neck and an expensive looking watch. Todd wondered how the kid could afford to dress so well if his mother was barely working.

"Does Jamal work?"

There was a moment of hesitation.

"Does Jamal have a job? On your application you put yourself down as the sole income for the family."

The woman turned to look at her son and she saw exactly what Todd had seen. There was no way she could lie.

"Ms. Watson?"

"He—He just has a little part-time job after school. It's nothing really. It's just so he can buy his school clothes." There was desperation in her voice.

"Where does he work?"

"UPS."

"My father used to work for UPS. They pay pretty well don't they? How much do you make, son?"

Todd saw the woman turn to her son and give him a look as if she were trying to will him to lie.

"Ten dollars an hour."

Todd scribbled some notes on their application. "Wow. That's pretty good. What do you do there?"

"I load boxes onto the trucks."

"That's good hard work there, son. That's man's work. You should be proud of yourself. My dad used to drive the forklift. How many hours a week do you work?"

Ms. Watson looked terrified. "Twenty, including weekends."

"So, you make about $200 a week?" The boy nodded.

Todd looked at the woman and shook his head.

"I'm sorry. But there's no way I can approve your application. With both of you working part-time you make too much money. Now I can approve you for WIC and maybe some food stamps but I can't give you a check."

"But that's not fair! I have a baby on the way. You're punishing me for working? So, if I was one of these lazy-ass bitches who just leeched off the system forever and never tried to make something of themselves then you'd approve me no problem then, huh? This is bullshit!"

She picked up her purse and prepared to leave. "Come on, kids."

Todd held up a hand and waved her back into her seat. "Wait. There might be something else I can do for you."

Ms. Watson turned and looked at him suspiciously then eased herself back down into the seat, letting the purse slip from her shoulder back into her lap.

"Look, you're going to school, trying to build yourself a career and give your kids a good life. I admire that. It's rare to see that sort of thing around here. That baby is only going to complicate things for you. If you'd consent to an abortion and then have a tubal ligation I'll forget about Jamal's job and qualify you for monthly assistance."

"What the fuck did you just say?"

"I know you're already in your second trimester but there are doctors who can still do it safely."

"I can't believe this shit. What is this? Some sort of government genocide program? Trying to sterilize all the niggers so we can't reproduce? Wipe us all out in a couple of generations?"

"No, I'm afraid you've misunderstood me."

"No. I understand you perfectly, White man! You want to kill my baby! You sick-ass peckerwood motherfucker!"

She was getting loud. Other people were starting to look over at Todd's cubicle.

"Please, calm down. Lower your voice."

"Why? You don't want all of these people to know what the government is up to? They are trying to bribe you to have an abortion! They don't want no more niggers being born!"

"This isn't a conspiracy. You just misunderstood me."

"I didn't misunderstand shit!"

Todd stood up and gestured toward security over the clear plastic wall of his cubicle. They were already on their way and when they saw Todd they rushed forward blocking the cubicle.

"Come with us, ma'am. We're going to have to ask you to leave the building."

"Don't fucking touch me! You'd better not touch me."

"No one is going to touch you."

"Come on, Jamal!"

She stormed out of Todd's cubicle, casting one last look over her shoulder at him.

Todd collapsed down into his chair. Shaken. There was a line of applicants standing outside his cubicle. He didn't know if he had the strength to face them.

"Todd? Are you okay?"

Todd looked up. It was his supervisor, Elizabeth Santiago. She was in her forties, attractive, though a bit overweight, with long curly black hair that came down to mid-back, large breasts and hips and a large ass that she seemed to be embarrassed of. She always wore skirts and a blazer and Todd had never seen her without her shirt buttoned all the way up to the top, regardless of the weather. She was the most uptight woman he'd ever met.

"Yes. I'm okay. I just need a moment. I'll be fine."

"Did she attack you?"

"No. I'm fine."

"What was that all about?"

"I found out that her son had a job and she hadn't disclosed that on her application. I had to turn her down and she got upset."

"Yeah, I'd say she was upset. What was all of that about the government wanting her to have an abortion?"

Todd shrugged his shoulders and looked down at his desk.

"I guess she thought that was her only option if she couldn't get welfare."

"These people. You'd think they'd consider all of that before they ran off and got themselves pregnant. There is such a thing as birth control." She shook her head and turned her back on Todd as she walked out of his cubicle.

For the rest of the day, Todd did his job as he had done it the last six years, but no more pregnant women had come in, so that had made it easier. He wasn't sure what he would have told the next pregnant woman who came in. He kept thinking about what Heimlich had said about one human being responsible for the death of 100 animals and the loss of over an acre of trees every year. He didn't know if it was in him to stand by and do nothing. Then Terrence Mohammed walked into his cubicle.

Terrence was a six-foot-seven, two-hundred and sixty-pound, former high school basketball star who had flunked out before graduation and ruined any chance he'd ever had of a college scholarship or ever entering the NBA. Now he was almost thirty and had four children by three different women. He wasn't married to any of them but he was paying child support to all three of them.

"I want to take care of my kids. I just don't know how I can take care of all of them and still feed myself."

Todd wondered how many children a guy like this could potentially produce in his lifetime. He could almost see all those millions of potential kids pooled in his scrotum, waiting to attack some unsuspecting ovum. Statistics from Heimlich's book began to run through Todd's head. The average adult male had 2.3 children, but if they didn't graduate from college they were 38% more likely to produce more than five children. Black men were 25% more likely than whites to produce more than four children in their lifetime. This man was a walking baby factory. Everything about him disgusted Todd. He imagined those old Catholic families that used to have twelve and thirteen kids. He shuddered visibly.

"I have a proposition for you that might just help you out." Todd smiled and Terrence smiled back at him.

"Have you ever considered having a vasectomy?"

"What? You mean cut my nuts off?"

"No. Not exactly. It's a procedure where they cut the vas deferentia or sperm ducts and then seal them with stitches or by cauterizing the ends. It's perfectly safe and these days there's very little pain and of course, you'd still be able to function sexually, just without the risk of unwanted children."

Terrence laughed.

"Man, you trippin'. You want me to let some fool cut into my nuts and stitch them bitches closed?"

"In a manner of speaking. It's perfectly safe and it will keep you from making any more babies that you can't afford to feed. If you go ahead and have the procedure, I'll go ahead and qualify you to receive government assistance and I might even forget about the warrant out for your arrest for back child support."

It was a bluff of course. Todd had no way of knowing if the man was current on his child support or not.

"Man, I pay my child support. I ain't one of them deadbeat dads. Ain't no warrants out for me. All my baby-mommas love my black ass. And what happens if I get married some day and my wife wants kids? What am I supposed to tell her? That I sold my nuts for a welfare check? Come on, dude. I ain't goin' out like that."

"Well, then I'm afraid there's not much I can do for you."

Todd was furious. He could barely look at the man. This guy already had four kids and he was seriously considering having more. Todd put together a plan in his head as quickly as he could.

29

He was sure that he was making mistakes, mistakes that would get him caught. But this was an emergency and risks had to be taken.

"I can offer you some job training and placement. Here's the address of a guy who's hiring sales trainees. They pay really well and you'll be drawing a paycheck while you're in training. You just need to go to his house today at six. If you're late or if you don't show up then just rip this address up. This guy has a pretty busy schedule and there are a lot of people trying out for this position. I'm going to put a good word in for you though, so if you show up you'll be almost guaranteed to get the job."

Todd picked up a sticky note and wrote down the address to his own apartment. He hesitated a moment, trying to decide if he was willing to take it to this level, not knowing what he would do if the big guy showed up on his doorstep. He handed him the paper and the big man took it then grabbed his hand and shook enthusiastically with a large smile plastered on his face. Todd could see why so many women had fallen for him. Terrence was startlingly handsome and his smile was warm and friendly. He was the type of guy that women wanted to sleep with and men wanted to be friends with. Todd almost felt guilty for what he was planning on doing to the guy.

"I'll be there. Don't worry about that. Thanks, man. Thanks for everything."

"My pleasure."

Todd watched the big man leave. He would need something to bring a guy that size down. Something he could use to control him with. He didn't have anything in his apartment that he thought could do the trick. He'd have to make a stop on the way home. There was a police supply store just a few blocks from the office where he knew he could get a stun gun and some handcuffs. Just a few blocks from there was a medical supply store where he could pick up a scalpel and some catgut for stitches. He wouldn't be able to get any painkillers without a prescription so he'd have to manage without them. He made a mental note to add duct tape to his list. He hoped this wouldn't be too expensive.

He turned over the sign outside his cubicle directing the remaining applicants to the next representative. He was going to take a ten minute break. He logged onto his computer and clicked on the search engine. He typed in "vasectomy step-by-step procedure" and began scribbling down notes.

Six

As Todd sat in his living room with the stun gun on his lap, handcuffs in one pocket and pepper spray and duct tape in the other, he had a moment to wonder about his sanity. The sun was already beginning to set and shadows crawled across the floor as Todd sat there, quietly contemplating how he would go about immobilizing a man he'd just met long enough to neuter him. He wondered if he was turning into some kind of psychotic madman.

It's not like I'm going to kill the guy. I'm just going to fix him. They don't call vets psychotic when they neuter dogs against their will. This is the same thing. Isn't it?

Todd wasn't exactly sure. What he was about to do was definitely not normal. But did it make him a monster? He knew that he had none of the major warning signs of a serial killer. He had never tortured animals, never set fires. He had wet the bed until he was ten though, and he had, technically, been abused by a domineering mother, though he had never thought of it as abuse. It wasn't like she'd fondled him or burnt him with cigarettes. She'd just had a firm hand when it came to discipline. Todd remembered the whippings across his back and thighs with twisted wire hangers and extension cords. Severe, perhaps, by modern standards but no more or less than any good parent would have done 50 years ago. She was a bit of a religious fanatic, never letting him play with other kids, making him read the Bible every day.

Oh my God. Maybe I am crazy?

He tried to console himself with the notion that crazy people didn't know they were crazy, so if he thought that he was going crazy then he must still be sane. It was slim comfort though. He couldn't bullshit himself.

No matter how convinced he was that this was the right thing to do, that Terrence Mohammed would have created more babies, perhaps even dozens more, that he wouldn't have been able to support and each of those children would have consumed more of the earth's resources and produced hundreds of tons of pollution and waste, Todd couldn't convince himself that the man deserved this. He looked over at the plastic he'd laid out on the kitchen floor. There was a scalpel, two forceps, a needle threaded with catgut and a disposable cigarette lighter.

What the fuck am I doing? How the hell am I going to cut open some guy's testicles?

There was a bottle of tequila on the kitchen counter that Todd had intended on using for a disinfectant. It was left over from his ex-girlfriend's birthday party in June. She'd drained the other bottle the night of the party and then ran off with a lesbian from the bail bonds office where she worked. She'd been mad at him because he hadn't wanted to get married and have kids. Before the argument had begun she'd had four margaritas and a couple shots of Patron and was already cozying up to her co-worker. Todd had had a few shots as well. When he'd shared with her his opinion of people who reproduced the entire room had gone silent.

"I think everyone should be gay. No one should ever procreate. Homosexuality may be a natural adaptation, nature's antidote to over-population. Anyone who reproduces when the world is already stretched way beyond its capacity is a selfish asshole."

"So, I'm a selfish asshole? I want kids."

"You can't be serious."

Tact had never been one of Todd's strong suits. His brutal honesty was one of the things Stephanie had liked about him in the beginning of their relationship but a mere four months later, she was already over it and it was the cause of many bitter disagreements. That night they argued, there were tears, harsh words and finally the door had slammed and he'd been alone. Her birthday party had probably not been the right place and time for that particular discussion.

Stephanie had been his first girlfriend. She was his polar opposite. She rode a Harley and worked as a bond agent/ bounty hunter. She was bisexual and had a body from hell. Large breasts courtesy of a skillful plastic surgeon, a hard muscular body from countless hours in the gym, long curly brown hair, full lips that always seemed to grin sarcastically as if she thought the world was a joke, and big fearful eyes as if she were afraid the joke was on her. Todd had tried his best not to question how a geek like him had managed such a catch because he knew that Stephanie was turned off by insecurity.

"I'm insecure enough for the both of us," she always said, and that, Todd supposed, answered his question. She was insecure and Todd was about as non-threatening as you could get. He'd still been a virgin when they met, whereas she had been anything but. He wondered what Stephanie would have thought about what he was about to do. She had always said that he was crazy but in a harmless and pitiful sort of way. Todd wondered if she would have still thought him harmless and pitiful. He had not seen Stephanie since their separation. He hoped she was happy, but more importantly, he was grateful that she wasn't breeding.

Todd walked over to the bottle and took another long swig, washing Stephanie from his mind. Fuck her. The past is the past.

The amber liquid burned its way down his throat and made his head feel hollow and light. Todd coughed a few times then turned the bottle up again, this time taking an even longer drink. The room tilted and Todd staggered a little. Thinking about Stephanie had messed with his head, as if his head wasn't screwed up enough by what he was about to do. He hated to drink but he needed something to help him through this. This wasn't the type of thing he could ask Heimlich for advice on, at least not in a public forum.

He wished that he had the man's personal email address. Instead, he would have to make up his own mind on this one. It was too late to punk out now. Terrence would be knocking on his door any minute. Todd only hoped that the stun gun would be enough to take the man down. He couldn't afford a gun and he didn't think that a knife would be threatening enough. The guy was so big that if Todd pulled a knife on him, he was afraid the guy would take it away from him and make him eat it. He'd have to ambush the big man and take him out quickly.

I must be fucking nuts, Todd thought. *I can't do this. There's no fucking way I can do this.*

Todd paced back and forth across the living room floor. He stopped and stared at the surgical tools for a long time, breathing heavily, heart racing, trying to imagine the type of pain the man would be in. It was unimaginable. He didn't know if he had it in him to continue if the guy were to wake up and start screaming. That would seriously freak him out. If only he could have gotten his hands on some type of narcotic, but Todd didn't have a prescription for anything and he didn't have enough money left over to try to score heroine even if he had known where to get it. With his luck he'd have only wound up getting his ass robbed and murdered trying to score some horse from the vatos.

Todd plopped down on the couch and checked his Timex. It was 6:06 pm. The guy was late. Perhaps he wouldn't show at all. Todd tried to relax but he was still too amped up. He bounced his legs up and down rapidly and wrung out his hands.

Where the fuck is this guy? Maybe he won't show? This was crazy anyway. There's no way I could have gone through with it. I wouldn't have done it anyway. I'm not that kind of person. This is just sick. I'm not crazy.

Todd looked back over at the surgical instruments on the floor. *If I wasn't really going to do it then why'd I buy all of that stuff?* He looked down at the stun gun in his hand and then back over at the scalpel and the forceps. He could probably return the stun gun and the handcuffs but the medical supply store had a no return policy. Todd's doorbell rang.

Well, I did pay for all of this. It would be a shame not to use it. He walked to the front door and opened it quickly.

"You're late."

"I know. I'm sorry. I know you told me not to be late but I had to wait for my mom to come home from work so I could use her car."

A look of confusion crossed the big man's face.

"What are you doing here anyway? Where's this guy I'm supposed to be meeting?"

Terrence looked over Todd's shoulder into the apartment. Todd hoped the big man couldn't see into the kitchen. If he saw the plastic on the floor with the scalpel on it he'd probably haul-ass out of there and call the cops. Then Todd would have a lot of explaining to do, first to the cops and then to his supervisor at work.

Todd stepped backwards into the apartment, leaving the door open for Terrence to follow. Terrence walked in, still looking at Todd, waiting for an answer. Todd smiled and the big basketball player smiled back. He really did have a great smile.

"I'm here to help."

Todd placed the stun gun against the big man's rib cage and pulled the trigger. The directions said to deliver a two-second burst. Todd held it there for a count of ten. Terrence dropped almost immediately. Todd stepped over him, kicked his legs out of the doorway and slammed the door shut. He quickly knelt down and handcuffed the big man, then he pulled out the duct tape and began taping his ankles together. Terrence was still disoriented but he was coming around quickly, rising to his knees, trying to struggle to his feet. He fell onto his face then tried to get up once more. Todd zapped him again. The man let out a sharp yell and fell over again, gritting his teeth against the pain. Saliva drooled out of both corners of his mouth. Todd finished taping his ankles, going around them four or five extra times just to make sure he couldn't break free. Then he stood up and wrapped Terrence's mouth in duct tape as well. The man awoke as Todd finished taping his mouth closed. He looked terrified.

"I'm sorry about all of this, Terrence. But you'll thank me someday. It's the right thing to do."

Todd pulled the big man's jeans down to his ankles. Terence's eyes widened and he began to thrash and scream against the tape. Todd had to zap him again.

I can't keep zapping him. I've got to find some other way of controlling him. Todd began wrapping tape around the big man's torso. He was mummifying him. He wrapped tape from Terrence's chest down to his hips. He grabbed

35

the big man's penis and taped it to his stomach. Terrence's cock was enormous. It stretched up past his navel. Todd felt a pang of jealousy. He wrapped it a few more times until it was completely covered, leaving only his testicles exposed. Todd grabbed another roll of tape and began taping up the big guy's legs. By then Terrence was awake again. It didn't matter now. He wasn't going anywhere.

Todd stood above Terrence, watching him squirm, waiting to make sure the man was completely helpless before he began to operate on him. Satisfied, he grabbed Terrence by the ankles and shuffled backward, dragging him toward the kitchen. He was even heavier than he looked. Todd had to drop the big man's legs and rest several times before he finally wrestled him onto the plastic.

Todd could hear his muffled moans and cries through the tape when the big man spotted the surgical tools. Terrence's eyes widened and wept tears. He shook his head back and forth and tried to struggle free but the tape immobilized him completely.

Todd picked up the bottle of Patron and took another swig, then he poured what was left of it on Terrence's testicles. Terrence writhed and shrieked.

"Oh, shit. I forgot that alcohol burns. Unfortunately, it's only going to get worse."

Todd picked up the scalpel and knelt down. He lifted Terrence's nut sack and the man's entire body tensed. He began making little jerking movements. He barely moved an inch despite what must have been a tremendous exertion. It was all he could manage with his body nearly mummified in duct tape.

"I would really advise you to stay still. I'm nervous as it is and it ain't like I do this shit every day. If I slip I might just cut your nuts off." The big guy stopped moving but began weeping and screaming against the tape again. Todd could barely hear him. The tape had done its job.

Todd cupped the man's scrotum in the palm of his hand and made one long incision in the thick wrinkly skin. Terrence's body vibrated as he continued to scream soundlessly. His head thrashed from side to side. Todd's hand began to shake.

"You're making me nervous!"

Todd cut another long incision on the other side of Terrence's nut sack. Then, he took a long breath and groped for the tequila bottle. It was empty. Todd fished his index finger into one of the slits in the big man's scrotum and pulled out the vas deferens, tiny white pinkish spermatic cords that led to his testicles. The man screamed and shook as Todd's hand groped around in his scrotum, fumbling with his testicles.

The amount of blood pouring out of him was far more than Todd had expected. It completely covered his hands.

I guess I should have gotten a bigger sheet of plastic.

Todd grabbed both of the clamps and attached them to one of the pinkish cords about an inch apart.

Shit. How do I know if this is the right one?

Todd looked at it and shrugged his shoulders. He picked up the scalpel and cut out the space between the two clamps. Then he picked up the needle, already threaded with cat gut, and stitched the two ends closed. Terrence was jerking and shaking again. Tears ran from his bulging eyes in a steady stream. Todd could scarcely imagine the pain the guy must have been in. He'd been kicked in the balls once and he'd nearly passed out, the pain had been so terrible. He remembered that sick nauseous feeling in the pit of his stomach and the taste of bile burning in his throat. He could not conceive how bad it must hurt to have someone cut into your nut sack and then clip the cords. He was surprised the guy was still conscious. He would have probably been better off if he wasn't.

"Alright big guy, I need to do the other one now."

Terrence thrashed his head back and forth with his pupils wide as golf balls. Todd reached into the big man's scrotum again and pulled out the next set of sperm cords. He put the clamps on them and Terrence's entire body shook and then went limp. The big guy had finally passed out. Todd shook his head sympathetically and brought the scalpel down once more.

Seven

The night of his wife's funeral, after everyone had finally gone home, Todd's father, Randy, was visited by the pastor of the church, the one who had performed the funeral service. Todd had thought it odd that the man hadn't come back to their house to eat like everyone else. He found it odder still that the man had come back after the other guests had gone.

The kitchen table was cluttered with Tupperware containers filled with food, casserole dishes covered with aluminum foil, plates of fried chicken, pies, cakes, and sympathy cards. Todd and his father were trying to find room for it all in the refrigerator when the doorbell rang. Todd watched his father shuffle wearily toward the front door. He looked through the peephole then unlocked the deadbolt and ushered the pastor into the apartment.

"Reverend James. Come on in."

Reverend James was young for a preacher. He couldn't have been older than forty. He had icy bluish gray eyes, black curly hair, dimpled cheeks, and a square jaw with full, almost feminine, lips. He was a beautiful man, beautiful in a way that made other men uncomfortable. Everyone in his congregation assumed that he was gay. Todd's father had made the same assumption. He was wrong.

The two men went into the kitchen and his dad made the reverend a cup of coffee. Then Todd was sent to his room. Todd was sitting on the floor playing with his transformers when the shouting started.

"You? You? You did this? And you had the nerve to preach at her funeral? You killed her! You sonuvabitch! You killed her!"

Todd could not hear the preacher's reply. He heard the wet smack and thud of flesh hitting flesh then furniture falling and breaking followed by a gunshot, a sick gurgling sound, another gunshot then the thud of something heavy hitting the floor, a long pause, followed by the sound of his father weeping.

"Oh shit. Oh shit. What did I do? I'm going to prison. How could you do this, Rachael? How could you do this to me?"

There was more silence, more tears, followed by whispering that Todd could not decipher. Then he heard the words that made him dart from his room and run toward the kitchen.

"I'm sorry, Toddy. I can't do it. I just can't do it. I can't go to prison. I can't live without your mom. I'm sorry."

Todd ran into the kitchen just as his father placed the gun in his mouth. Todd saw the priest's body lying on the floor with the hands clenching and unclenching and the legs bicycling slowly as if the man was still trying to run, only half his skull was missing and he wasn't going anywhere. Blood pumped out of what was left of the man's face. Todd looked back at his father. A single tear raced down his cheek and then he seemed to smile, even with the Desert Eagle .50 cal. filling his mouth. He closed his eyes and pulled the trigger. Todd closed his eyes too. He stood there in the kitchen with two bodies twitching on the floor beside him and blood pooling at his feet for the second time in less than a week. Todd was an orphan now. He was all alone. He turned and walked out of the room and this time he did not cry.

Eight

Todd had just finished stitching up Terrence's scrotum when the big man woke up. The big basketball player began screaming immediately, writhing on the floor in agony. Only then did it occur to Todd that he had no idea what to do with the man now that the surgery was complete. If he just let the big man go he would go straight to the police and Todd would be arrested and put in prison.

Todd sat beside him on the floor watching the man tremble and convulse. The man's enormous cock had shriveled up like a cocktail weenie and blood continued to weep through the stitches in his ball-sack.

"What do I do now?"

He couldn't even remove the guy's gag unless he wanted the neighbors to call the cops when the man started screaming his head off. Todd knelt over Terrence and cupped the man's face between his hands, looking him in his eyes.

"This was for your own good. I did this for you, for all of us. You can't afford the kids you have already. You shouldn't be having more. This world can't afford any more. The world is dying. Don't you see that? There are just too many people."

Terrence's eyebrows knit together and his face twisted into an enraged scowl. His eyes flashed brilliant with anger. He shook his head violently, trying to free it from Todd's hands. Todd looked up at the ceiling and tried to gather his thoughts, to find the words to make the big man understand.

"Do you know that it took hundreds of thousands of years for the world's population to reach one billion and in

40

the 200 years that followed, it has more than quintupled? The world's population has tripled since 1980, to 6 billion people, and is expected to grow to 9 billion by 2050. For every one of those 6 billion people on Earth nearly six tons of carbon dioxide is spewed into the air annually. Do you realize that one human being generates over 1,569 pounds of waste a year? That's nearly 125,000 pounds in a lifetime, sixty-two tons! And that's just one person! Half of the land on the earth has already been built on, paved over, and otherwise altered so that it is almost uninhabitable by any species other than humans and the insects and vermin that thrive off of us. And as the population continues to grow we'll need to convert even more land into habitable space for humans, meaning inhabitable space for almost everything else. How can we allow that? Fifty percent of the world's original forests have been destroyed as a result of massive land clearing for housing, roads, agriculture, and industries. Do you get what I'm saying? Do you even give a fuck? Your sperm cells are destroying the planet! So, I had to stop you. I had to stop you from reproducing."

Todd paused and stared into Terrence's eyes. There was no understanding there, just a white-hot rage and fear. He was looking at Todd the way you would look at a kid on Ritalin who'd just taken a loaded shotgun down from the mantle. He looked terrified.

"You don't care do you? Nobody cares."

Todd dropped Terrence's head hard onto the plastic covered vinyl floor and stormed out of the room. Terrence's eyes rolled up into his head as he passed out once again. Todd stomped into his bedroom, slammed the door and flicked on the television. He paced back and forth in his tiny little room. He grinded his teeth and tears rolled from his eyes. Several times he yelled or screamed. The tears came more forcefully and so did his rage.

"He doesn't understand. He's going to tell the police. What am I going to do? What the fuck am I going to do?"

He punched himself in the head several times as he continued to yell and curse.

"Fuck! Fuck! What did I do? What the fuck is wrong with me?"

41

He walked into the adjoining bathroom, looked at himself in the mirror, and once again doubted his sanity. There were a few smears of blood on his face from where he must have forgotten and touched it with his bloody hands. His clothes were matted with Terrence's blood and his hands and fingernails were caked with it. He looked like a murderer, a madman. He peeled off his clothes and climbed into the shower. The warm spray splashed onto his chest. Todd stood there, staring at the tiled wall, trying to collect his thoughts.

I've got to kill him.

It was a simple sobering thought.

I can't let him go now. I've got so much more to do. He'll ruin everything.

Todd stepped out of the shower and turned it off. He began to shiver as the cool conditioned air hit his warm skin. He didn't bother to put any clothes on. There was no need to ruin any more clothes with Terrence's blood. He walked back into the living room and into the kitchen. Terrence was awake again. He took one look at Todd and began to thrash and shake his head. Todd wondered for a second why he was reacting so violently. He didn't have any weapons on him yet. Then he remembered that he was naked. He looked down at himself and realized to his own embarrassment that he had an erection.

God, this guy must think I'm some kind of pervert.

"Don't worry; I'm not going to fuck you. I'm straight."

Terrence continued to shake his head back and forth, staring at Todd's erect cock like it was the barrel of a gun.

"Oh Jesus, are you serious? Calm down. I'm not going to do anything to you. I'm straight! I'm not gay! Oh, fuck it."

Todd stepped over Terrence, noting that the man was probably getting an unwanted glimpse of his asshole and nut sack as he reached across the kitchen counter for the carving knife in the knife rack. He picked it up and looked at it. It was about seven inches long with a serrated edge. Just the thought of using that knife to saw through the big guy's flesh made Todd's stomach do a little flip. He was still straddling him and so the guy was still freaking out at the sight of Todd's naked genitalia. Todd stepped his other leg over him and put the knife back into the rack. There was no way he could have used that thing. Instead, he picked up the cleaver.

Nice and quick.

Terrence had somehow managed to loosen up the tape around his mouth with all the thrashing around he'd been doing.

"Heeeeelp! Don't fucking come near me. Don't you fucking touch me, you sick ass crazy motherfucker!"

Todd brought the cleaver down on Terrence's throat. The blade cut through the big man's esophagus and lodged in his cervical vertebrae. Terrence's body began to tremble and shake. Blood sprayed from the wound in his neck and bubbled up from his mouth. A gurgling, whistling, wheezing sound came from the gash in the big guy's lacerated throat. The chords in his neck bulged as if he were trying to scream. It had not been the quick cut Todd had been expecting. He had hoped to behead him.

It took a bit of effort to dislodge the cleaver from Terrence's neck. There was a sickening wet ripping and cracking sound as Todd yanked the blade free in an explosion of bright red arterial blood erupting from the big man's jugular and carotid arteries which had both been severed. Todd turned his head as his stomach finally betrayed him and he regurgitated onto the plastic, depositing the vegetarian burrito he'd had for lunch into the pool of blood.

Oh, God. This is fucking horrible. Oh, my God. I can't believe I killed the guy. It had to be done. I had no choice. It had to be done.

Terrence was still making those gurgling sounds. His eyes were completely dilated and his lips were moving as if he were trying to speak. His hands were still cuffed behind him and his arms duct taped to his sides but Todd could hear the man's fingers raking the plastic. Todd's stomach heaved again and more of its contents erupted from his throat. Todd kept his head turned as he brought the cleaver down again and again tossing blood into the air each time he wrenched it free for another blow. The wet sticky crack of the cleaver striking flesh, blood, and bone was making Todd's stomach do flip-flops. The bile continued to rise in Todd's throat. His throat was raw and scalded from swallowing it back down. Finally, he stood up and grabbed the serrated knife

43

from the knife rack and sawed the rest of the way through Terrence's vertebrae. Thankfully, the man was dead by then. Terrence's head rolled off the plastic and bounced against the refrigerator.

Todd stared at it. That warm inviting smile that had wooed so many women into having his children was nowhere in evidence. The man had died in terror and agony and it showed in the rictus on his face. Todd stood up slowly on wobbly legs. He was shaken and physically and mentally exhausted. He stepped over the big man's corpse and staggered back into his bedroom. His body was completely covered in blood but at least he hadn't ruined more of his clothes. He'd have to figure out what to do with his clothes as well as the body in the morning. Right now he was exhausted. He needed some sleep.

As Todd stepped out of the shower, dried off and climbed under the sheets, he wondered about his ability to sleep with a man's castrated and beheaded body exsanguinating on his kitchen floor. Surely that had to mean he was crazy. Only a psychopath or some sort of sociopath could sleep after something like that, with a dead man in the next room. Todd was too tired to give the question much consideration. He closed his eyes and drifted off, dreaming about his mother's bleeding vagina and his father's ruptured skull just like he always did. They were the only dreams he ever had.

Nine

The sun intruded into Todd's bedroom, waking him from a sleep filled with gore-streaked nightmares of pain and death. Perspiration trickled down his forehead into his eyes. He wiped it away with the back of his hand, squinting against the sunlight. His head felt fuzzy and sluggish as if he were waking from an all-night drinking binge. He remembered all the tequila he'd drank the night before just as the headache split through his skull. Seconds later his alarm clock went off. Todd smacked it off the night stand. It continued to blare. Clamping his hands over his ears he stood up and stepped on the clock with his bare foot. The alarm went off and the radio came on. Todd stomped down on it again and again, crushing it into silence. His headache was pounding now, throbbing in his temples.

Todd looked around the room, trying to reorient himself. He half expected to see his father's corpse with the skull caved in on one side lying against the wall across the room, the dead priest, chest hollowed out with one bullet, skull collapsed by another, his mother, still bleeding from her vagina, and Terrence Mohammed's headless body. But all he saw was his Sierra Club Earth Day posters and posters of Jim Morrison, R.E.M. and Kurt Cobain, his CD collection, the wall-mounted Sharper Image CD player, stacks of magazines, milk crates filled with books, the futon he slept on with the shattered radio/alarm clock alongside it and the pictures of his mom and dad and his dog Honey that sat on the night stand by his bed. Todd dressed quickly for work, still trying to shake off his headache, the previous nights blood-spattered dreams still echoing in his mind.

45

After he was dressed, Todd sat down on his bed and opened his laptop. He needed to connect with other like-minded individuals, others who understood the cause. He needed to talk to Heimlich.

Todd clicked on the link in his favorites to the Zero Population messageboard and a message popped up stating that the link could not be found. He tried it again several times and then tried the link to the Zero Population website. That was gone too.

"What the fuck is going on?"

Todd clicked onto a search engine and typed in Zero Population. The first thing that came up, at the top of the page, was today's headline, "Heimlich Anatolli Arrested for Terrorism." Todd clicked on the link to the story.

October 16th 2009, New York City, New York, Dr. Heimlich Anatolli, Biology Professor at MacDonald University and author of the controversial book Zero Population was arrested today when he and a group of university students attempted to poison New York City's water supply with an experimental sterility drug called Progesterex. Ironically, Heimlich was one of the inventors of the controversial drug marketed as a non-surgical alternative to tubal ligation surgery.

In a written statement given to police investigators, Dr. Anatolli cited overpopulation and the resultant "terminal damage to the ecosystem" as his reason for the attack. In the same statement, he indicated that, if successful, it would have been the beginning of a worldwide campaign targeting 25 of the most populous cities in the world including Los Angeles, Mumbai, Sao Paolo, Mexico City, Hong Kong, Tokyo, and Osaka. According to researchers, this would have resulted in the involuntary sterilization of nearly 300 million women. "His efforts would have reduced population growth by more than half. It might have been just what the environment needed," said one prominent Socio-Anthropologist who asked not to be identified. In his statement, Dr. Anatolli was quoted as saying, "My only regret is that I failed. Hopefully someone else will carry on my work or else we're all doomed."

Dr. Anatolli will be arraigned today on charges of terrorism and 10 million counts of aggravated assault.

Todd could barely believe what he was reading. He clicked on several other articles but none of them contained any more details. Todd was alone now. His mentor had been captured. All hope was lost. Somehow, Todd had to get his hands on the drug and continue the man's work. He Googled Progesterex and could find no one in America who sold the drug. There was a factory in Beijing that manufactured it but they could no longer legally export it to America.

"There has to be a way."

Todd continued searching the web for another hour until he had to leave for work. He found out everything about the drug except how to acquire it. It had originally been marketed as a hormonal therapy drug for chemotherapy patients only to be discontinued when it was discovered that it reduced the amount of estrogen and progesterone the body produces, sending women into early menopause and rendering them infertile. Heimlich had gotten a grant to continue research on the drug as a safe and permanent form of birth control, a non-surgical alternative to tubal ligation. Obviously, he had perfected it.

The kitchen was a mess. Luckily Todd was already running late for work so there was no time for breakfast even if he'd had the stomach for it. Todd could not believe that he had left it this way. If anyone were to have peeked into his apartment he'd have been on death row in a heartbeat. Terrence's body still lay on the plastic where he had left it.

The blood had finally coagulated and hardened in places to a brownish red crust. The man's head was still lying against the refrigerator. Todd considered finishing the job of hacking his body up for disposal, but could think of no way to do it that wouldn't have ruined his clothes and made him even later. Terrence would have to wait until after work.

The big man's body would have to be cut into pieces small enough to haul off in his messenger bag, unless he could borrow someone's car. That was going to take a lot of work. He wondered if he could call Stephanie and ask to use her car. He hadn't spoken more than a couple of words to her since they'd broken up five months ago. Calling her to use her car probably wouldn't go over too well.

Todd looked down at the man and felt a pang of guilt and sorrow. He had murdered another human being. He had not just prevented him from having other kids. He had taken the man away from his existing kids, the kids he had been supporting. They would now grow up fatherless because of Todd.

This isn't what I wanted. Things just got out of control. I'll be more careful next time.

And there would be a next time. Todd couldn't fool himself about that. He was fully committed now. Now that Heimlich was in prison, it was all up to him.

Todd picked up the scalpel from the floor and put it in his messenger bag. He grabbed the last two remaining rolls of duct tape from the four-pack he'd bought at the hardware store. He considered trying to roll Terrence over and retrieve the handcuffs but he couldn't think of any way to do it that wouldn't get his clothes bloody, so instead he picked up the clamps and the stun gun where he'd left it by the couch in the living room and grabbed his bike from where it stood by the front door.

Locking the door behind him, Todd carried his bike down the stairs to the street. As he rode to work, passing cars locked in traffic, belching noxious fumes into the air and coffee shops and breakfast joints filled with chain-smoking consumers destroying the earth one Styrofoam cup and sausage and egg biscuit at a time, Todd's sense of urgency increased.

They have got to be stopped.

Ten

Todd had no stomach for the job today. The endless line of needy people had no concept of what real poverty was. In America, the average "poor person" had a color TV, a DVD player, a microwave oven, and a car. People in third world countries, who lived without running water, refrigeration, heat or electricity, would be justifiably offended by the things Todd saw every day. His first applicant of the day had come in wearing diamond earrings and a platinum necklace. In six years Todd had still not gotten used to the astounding gall of some people.

He wasn't in the mood to fight it today. Todd was still exhausted and, despite taking a fistful of Extra-Strength Tylenol, his head still throbbed with a dull ache. Today, Todd rubber-stamped every application that came in with the exception of one or two obvious cases of fraud. He was too tired to argue with anyone. Then Nicolene came in.

She looked much the same as she had two days ago. Still pregnant. Still strung-out. Only now she was alone.

"Michael's dead. Some guy…a trick…picked him up yesterday and gave him some dope that was uncut. When Michael started convulsing, the guy dumped him in an alley. By the time someone noticed him back there and called the ambulance he was already dead."

"I'm sorry to hear that." Todd looked down at her belly. "So, what are your plans now?"

"I'm not having an abortion. I just wanted to tell you that. I'm keeping my baby. And I'm not getting myself fixed either. I'm going to get clean. I signed up for one of those

Narcotics Anonymous programs. I'm going to kick. I'm going to be a good mom."

Todd was furious. He glared at her without saying a word.

"I need to get on welfare. You can't turn me down. I qualify."

"Are you sure you want to do this? Most of the baby's brain and spine development happens in the first two trimesters. That child might already be messed up."

Nicolene tilted up her head defiantly. She rubbed her hands over her belly then looked down at it and smiled.

"I don't care. This is all I have left of Michael and I'm keeping it. And if you don't get me that assistance I'm going to tell everyone about how you tried to force me to have an abortion."

Todd looked at the messenger bag sitting next to his filing cabinet.

"Very well then. Which address would you like it sent to?"

Nicolene smiled, satisfied. Todd smiled too. As high as she was, some latent self-preservation instinct still told her that there was something not quite right about that smile. It was perhaps an instinct she had picked up from her many months turning tricks on the streets. She had gotten good at spotting the bad ones and if Todd had pulled up beside her wearing a smile like that, there was no way she would have gotten into his car.

"The one on the application. That's where I live."

"Good."

Todd stamped the application approved and placed it in a pile on his desk.

"You can expect your first check in six to eight weeks."

"Thank you."

Nicolene backed slowly out of Todd's cubicle as if she were afraid to turn her back on him. Then she turned quickly and started to walk away.

"See you soon," he whispered.

Nicolene turned back and looked at him. He was still wearing that creepy smile. She turned away and hurried out of the building.

Eleven

Todd had almost forgotten about Terrence's body as he rode home. He almost rode right past the hardware store until he remembered that he would need a hacksaw and an axe. He went into the store and felt as if all eyes were on him. He didn't know a hell of a lot about serial killers so he didn't know if buying the axe would be suspicious. He decided not to risk it by including a bag of lye. Perhaps he could get that from some other store like Home Depot where everyone would be too busy to notice him. A mom and pop store like this would probably remember every last detail of his purchase, but Home Depot was another ten miles away and he was already tired. Plus, the longer he left Terrence's body in his apartment the more likely it was that it would start stinking and he'd be discovered. He'd just have to do without the lye.

When he walked up to the counter with the contractor grade trash bags, the axe, and the hacksaw, he was almost positive that the cashier would hit some type of alarm and have him arrested. He had to keep telling himself that it only seemed suspicious to him because he knew what he'd done. To anyone else, he was just a guy buying tools. People purchased axes and hacksaws every day without using them to dismember corpses.

"Chopping down a tree?"

"Excuse me?"

The cashier, an old man in his sixties who probably owned the place, pointed at the axe.

"The axe. You got yourself a tree to chop down?"

Todd stared at the man, trying to figure out how to reply and realizing that each second he went without answering made him look more and more suspicious.

51

"Uh, no. I'm chopping firewood. I've got a wood stove."

"Then you don't want that axe. I got a better one back there that'll split wood into kindling with one swing."

"Th-This one will be fine."

"It ain't much more expensive."

"I'm on a budget."

"A little hot out to be burning wood?"

"I've got a cabin up at Mammoth Mountain. I'm going there for the weekend."

The old guy began ringing up Todd's order.

"You should go up to Big Bear. It's beautiful up there. I saw Sugar Ray Leonard up there once. He was just jogging on the road. It was right before his fight with Roberto Duran. I ain't never been to Mammoth Mountain though. I never was much into skiing. I was always more of a hunter."

Todd bristled.

"Good for you." he said through clenched teeth.

"Oh, I see. You're one of them tree huggers. Well, you have fun up at your cabin doing whatever you guys do up there."

Todd paid the man for the tools, picked up his bags, and walked out of the store. He had wanted to call the old man a murderer but somehow, no longer felt like he had the right.

It felt as if every eye was on him as he rode his bike back to the apartment. Every time he passed a police cruiser his pulse-rate shot up, his chest tightened, and he began to perspire.

I thought sociopaths weren't supposed to have normal fear responses? I'm scared to fucking death. If this isn't normal I'd hate to feel what normal people feel.

Twice during the ride home he turned off of the main road onto a side street, convinced that he was being followed by the police. It took him more than half an hour to travel what normally took him less than twenty minutes.

Todd wrestled his bike and the messenger bag filled with tools up to his apartment. Pausing outside the front door, Todd inhaled deeply, collecting himself before confronting his gruesome task. He wasn't sure if it was just his imagination or not, but he thought he could smell Terrence's blood from outside the apartment. He could definitely smell something. The apartment smelled like a public toilet. The corpse had voided its waste after he'd beheaded it and Todd hadn't bothered to clean that up either. He stood outside the front door running the entire process over and over in his head. It was inconceivable. He couldn't wrap his head around it.

"Fuck it. There's nothing to it but to do it, I guess."

Todd opened the door. Terrence Mohammed's body lay exactly where he'd left it. The man was huge. It would take him forever to cut him into small enough pieces to fit into his messenger bag and then it would take him a dozen trips or more to haul it all away. He needed a car. He had to call Stephanie. She was the closest thing he'd ever had to a friend and even if she thought he was an asshole now, she still might help him out. He pulled the hacksaw out of the bag, knelt down on top of Terrence's chest, lifted his arm, and began sawing through his armpit joint. Halfway through the joint he picked up his cell phone and dialed Stephanie's number for the first time in months.

"Hello?"

"Stephanie?"

"Who is this?"

"It's Todd."

"Todd? Oh. How've you been?"

"I'm okay. I'm good. How're you doin'?"

"I...well...I'm doin' pretty well. I'm all right. So, what's up? What's that noise?"

"I'm chopping some meat."

"You? Meat?"

"It's for a friend."

Todd sawed the arm off and began wrapping it up in plastic. "So, what's going on, Todd? I haven't heard from you in forever."

"Five months."

"What?"

"It's been five months."

"Okay, I haven't seen you in five months."

"Stephanie, I know this is going to sound weird, but I need to borrow your car."

There was a long silence on the other end of the phone. "Stephanie?"

"I thought you didn't believe in cars? You told me that I was killing the planet when I bought my car. I bought a fucking Prius because of you and even that wasn't good enough. You in some kind of trouble?"

"I just need to borrow it for about an hour or two."

"You're not going on a date are you? Because that would be fucking tacky, using your ex-girlfriend's car to pick up chicks."

"It's not for a date. I still love you."

"Todd…"

"I know. I know. I just need to borrow it to move some things into storage. I didn't know who else to call."

"Okay. Okay, Todd. Come by around ten. I've got to do a job first. Some scumbag raped his next-door neighbor and then skipped out on five hundred thousand dollars bail. I know where he's at so it shouldn't take long."

"Be careful."

"Cathy and I've been taking Muay Thai and Ju-jitsu. I'm pretty sure I can handle things if they get rough."

"I'm sure you can. See you at ten."

"Later."

Todd hung up the phone and lifted Terrence's leg. His legs were so long that he'd have to cut them in at least three pieces. He picked up the axe and brought it down hard on Terrence's kneecap, cutting deep into the joint. He wrenched it free and then brought it down again, this time cutting clean through the patella and tendons. He grabbed the basketball player's other leg and hefted the axe again. Todd took a moment to wonder how he'd thrown up cutting the man's head off only a day before. Now, he was hacking at the man's kneecap with an axe without hesitation.

He chopped off the feet and then went to work on the hip-joint, trying to remove his femur. He barely used the hacksaw at all as he continued dismantling Terrence's corpse and wrapped up each severed limb in plastic and duct tape.

When Todd was done, he had a dozen different pieces neatly wrapped on his living room floor. He'd quartered the big man's torso and wrapped each piece individually. Terrence's head was the only thing remaining to be wrapped. Todd tucked the man's head in a garbage bag and went around it several times with the duct tape. He looked at his watch. It was only six thirty. He still had time to catch Nicolene and ride to Stephanie's to pick up the car and dispose of Terrence's body.

Todd took another half hour to clean the kitchen floor, clean the blood that had spattered onto the walls, cabinets, carpet, and even the ceiling, roll up the bloodstained plastic and shove it into a trash bag. He washed the cleaver and the serrated carving knife and put them both in the dishwasher, then he mopped the floor with ammonia. The house looked almost normal except for the body parts wrapped in plastic and piled on his living room floor. Terrence's clothes also sat in a bloody pile on the floor. Todd picked them up and a set of keys fell out of Terrence's basketball shorts.

Of course, Terrence must have driven here. He'd said that he'd borrowed his mother's car. That could be a problem. His mother would want her car back soon. Hopefully she wouldn't report it stolen if she still thought her son was driving it but you never know. People had some strange relationships with their parents these days.

Todd considered calling Stephanie back and telling her he didn't need the car. Trying to locate Terrence's car shouldn't have been too hard. But it would take some time and he was in a rush, besides, he really wanted to see Stephanie again and the car gave him the perfect excuse. He would have to find Terrence's car soon though. It wouldn't be long before he was reported missing and the car would be the first thing that the cops looked for. That was even more reason why he shouldn't use it to transport the man's body. If Todd got caught with the car he could probably talk his way out of it. If he got caught with the car filled with dismembered body parts, he was fucked.

He walked into his bedroom and picked up his laptop. He clicked on the search engine and typed in "tubal ligation, step by step procedure." It was too much to write down. He needed his printer. Todd plugged the laptop into his printer and began printing out an online medical manual.

When he was done he snatched up the papers and tucked them under his arm. Todd picked up the messenger bag containing the scalpel, forceps, tape, plastic, handcuffs and stun gun. He shoved the medical manual in there as well, then grabbed his bike and started down the stairs. He had a lot of work to do tonight…in honor of Heimlich. Only this time he'd have to make sure he wasn't seen. He didn't want to have to kill anyone else.

Twelve

Nicolene's neighborhood was not the type of place where a red-headed white boy on a ten-speed could feel safe. It was a mostly Black and Latino area, low-income, high-crime. Crackheads, alcoholics, and schizophrenics wandered the sidewalk mumbling to themselves, and kids as young as six and seven prowled the streets looking for some way to amuse themselves, which included smashing windows with rocks, breaking into cars to steal radios and CDs, and fighting amongst themselves.

There was a liquor store on the corner with a group of teenage thugs camped out in front of it. Two ambulances and ten police cars raced by within the first ten minutes that Todd had been there. Off in the distances he could hear the occasional gunshot. Hip-hop music competed with Salsa and Heavy Metal for aural dominance, blasting from passing cars and nearby houses and apartments. Many of the houses had boarded up windows including the apartment complex where Nicolene lived, no doubt the result of rocks from bored adolescents.

Todd waited across the street in an empty lot, leaning up against the rusted hulk of an old car. His bike leaned against the car beside him. He had it chained to the car's door through one of the missing windows. He'd also removed the seat and the front wheel and chained them to the frame. This would make his get-away much slower if he had to flee for any reason but he had no choice. If he'd left it unchained the seven-year-olds would have absconded with it in seconds.

The darker the night got, the less safe Todd felt. The noises of violence increased with the lateness of the hour.

Sounds of breaking glass, shouts, laughter, curses, and fist fights, echoed from behind closed doors. The good thing was that, even if Nicolene screamed when he grabbed her, he didn't think anyone would notice amid the already deafening cacophony of violence booming through the streets. Todd glanced up and down the block, nervously turning the stun gun in his pocket, fingering the trigger. He didn't have to wait as long as he'd thought.

Nicolene came staggering down the street with her bloated belly sticking out from beneath a tight black baby-t with "Hustler" silkscreened on the front of it. Even from across the street, Todd could see the white streaks on the front of the shirt. It didn't take a genius to figure out were from her last trick. Obviously Nicolene didn't swallow.

She staggered down the street grinning stupidly, in a narcotic fugue. She didn't even notice Todd stalking her, slipping through the door behind her as she let herself into her apartment building. She was babbling to herself as she walked up the piss-stained steps to her apartment. She'd already unlocked her door when she finally noticed Todd behind her. She whirled around with a switchblade in her hand, preparing to cut him when Todd hit her with the stun gun, knocking her off her feet. She was out cold and she hadn't seen him. So far, everything was going as planned.

Moving Nicolene's emaciated drug-ravaged body into her apartment was a hell of a lot easier than it had been moving Terrence's gigantic frame. He tossed her waifish body over his shoulder, stepped into the apartment, and kicked the door closed behind him. She was still unconscious. Todd pulled out the roll of duct tape and gagged her before he began binding her arms and legs. He rolled out the plastic on the kitchen floor and laid Nicolene down onto it, bumping her head as he dropped her the last four or five inches rather than risk his back by trying to lower her all the way to the floor. Nicolene's eyelids fluttered but remained closed. Then he reached into his messenger bag and removed the scalpel. This would be so much worse than what he'd done to Terrence, but it had to be done. She had to be stopped. Her baby could be the one to doom us all.

Once again, Todd would be operating with no anesthesia.

57

He grabbed the second roll of tape and went around her arms again, taping all the way up her shoulders to her neck. Then he went back down to her ankles and wrapped the tape up her legs to her hips. There was no way for her to move now. No way for her to struggle. He used one last piece of tape to blindfold her. She would have no idea what was happening to her or who was doing it. Todd awkwardly undressed and place his clothes on the kitchen counter. His clothes couldn't be soaked in blood when he saw Stephanie later.

Nicolene's chest heaved and her body jerked with the first cut. Todd made a low transverse incision from one side of her belly to the other, as Nicolene arched her back, screaming and writhing in agony. He cut through the subcutaneous fibrous muscle tissue of her abdominal wall that held her organs and abdominal muscles in place, and bubbles of yellow fat bulged outward and blood flooded the wound. Nicolene thrashed and convulsed, but the tape held her tight and limited her movement. He had not put as much tape on her as he had used on Terrence because he needed access to her stomach. That meant she had much more freedom of movement. Todd had to try to hold her down with one arm while cutting with the other. His incision was jagged and crooked, unable to keep his hand steady through Nicolene's frantic undulations.

Even through all the tape he'd wrapped around her mouth, her screams were terrible. Tears wept out from beneath the tape over her eyes. Todd cut deeper into her abdominal muscles and then pushed the muscle aside, revealing a thin layer of tissue covering her uterus. Nicolene's body trembled but she had stopped convulsing. Her breathing was coming short and quick. She was in shock. He had to hurry before he accidentally killed her. Hopefully, she had enough drugs in her already to numb much of the pain.

Todd made an incision in her peritoneum and lifted it away. Then he peeled her bladder away from her uterus. He was now kneeling in a river of blood. It covered his arms past the elbows. He wasn't sure how Nicolene could possibly survive this.

Several times he thought her heart had stopped and he paused to check her pulse. Occasionally, she would wake up and begin screaming again. That's when Todd would feel the bile rise in his throat as his stomach threatened to disgorge its contents. Todd closed his eyes for a moment and tried to calm his breathing. Nicolene began screaming again as he made an incision in her uterus. He stuck two fingers inside the incision and spread it wide. Amniotic fluid poured out onto the plastic, along with more blood. He could see the baby now. It was already head down, in the birthing position. He cupped a hand under its head and pushed down on Nicolene's stomach with the other hand pushing it out of her with one hand and dragging it out with the other. There was a loud *Slooorp!* as the baby ripped free of its mother and air rushed into the cavity where it had been.

Todd held the baby up and looked at it. A boy. Todd smiled. Then he calmly wrapped the umbilical cord around its neck and strangled it to death. It took several long minutes before the baby finally ceased to breathe. Todd began to weep.

What have I done? This is…this is horrible. What have I done?

But he wasn't done yet. Todd cut the umbilical cord and tossed the baby into the waste basket under the kitchen sink, then he reached back inside of Nicolene and groped for her fallopian tubes. He wasn't sure where to find them from this vantage point. Nicolene woke up again while his hands were inside of her. She began to buck and thrash and scream. Todd pulled his hands out of her and reached for the stun gun. He gave her a five second burst that knocked her unconscious once again. He checked her pulse again and she was still alive. Whatever drugs she had taken tonight were dulling the pain just enough to ward off terminal shock.

Todd found what he believed to be her fallopian tubes. He pulled them out of the incision so that he could see them better then looked at the papers he'd printed out on tubal ligation surgery. They were almost completely covered in blood. Unreadable. He shrugged his shoulders and then tied the tubes in a knot. He then cut out the center of the knot, took his Bic lighter, and cauterized both ends. He paused to wipe the sweat from his brow, smearing a dripping wet mask of blood over his face. He grimaced and then reached in for the other fallopian tube, repeating the process. When he was done, he paused to look at his work. Nicolene was awake again and flopping on the floor like a fish. Her bladder and her intestines were hanging out of her. Todd looked at the medical manual he'd printed out. It was now completely saturated in blood and fluids. He had to put her back together.

He peeled the pages apart as best he could and tried reading the few sentences that were still legible. Most of the pictures were still discernible even if the words were completely obscured. That would have to be enough. He pulled the uterus out of her abdominal cavity and picked up the needle threaded with catgut. He made a few neat stitches to close the incision he'd made in her uterus and then placed it back inside of her. Then he stitched her bladder back onto her uterus where he estimated it had been before he'd peeled them apart. Todd stretched the peritoneum back over her uterus and stitched that in place as well. He pulled the muscles back into place and made a couple of stitches to secure them. He had no idea if he'd done it right. It at least resembled what he could make out of the pictures. Lastly, Todd sewed her stomach closed.

Nicolene lay completely still now, barely breathing. Her body had finally succumbed to the pain. Todd stood up and washed his face and grabbed a sponge from beside the sink to clean the rest of his body. Once satisfied that he was passably clean, he dressed. He picked up the phone and dialed 911.

"There's a woman bleeding on the floor in here. I think she's dying. You'd better come quick."

Todd looked down at Nicolene. Blood leaked from her incisions. He didn't have so much as a band-aid to put on the wound. He'd have to be more prepared next time. Todd dropped the phone and left it off the hook so the paramedics could trace the call. He picked up all of his instruments and put them back into his messenger bag then walked out of the apartment, smiling. He felt like he had gotten it right this time. Now all he had to do was dispose of Terrence and his life could go back to normal.

Thirteen

Stephanie paced the floor from the kitchen to the front door to the window overlooking the street, wringing her hands and rubbing her belly and sighing deeply. Her girlfriend, Cathy, watched her angrily, fighting to remain silent. When Stephanie looked out the window for the tenth time in less than two minutes, Cathy could no longer remain silent.

"Why did you even invite him over if it's freaking you out so much?"

"He needed the car."

"So? Tell him to get his own damn car. What does he need a car for anyway?"

"I don't know. He said he needed to move some boxes or something."

"I hope he's not doing anything illegal."

"Todd? Please. He wouldn't hurt a fly. And I mean he literally would not hurt a fly."

Stephanie rubbed her belly again and then glanced out the window once more.

"You never told him huh?"

"How could I, knowing how he feels about it?"

"I can hand him the keys for you if you'd like. You don't have to see him. He doesn't have to see you."

"What will you tell him?"

"I don't have to tell him shit. He's the one who fucked up. You're my woman now. I'll just tell him you don't want to see him."

"You sound like a male chauvinist when you say I'm your woman."

"You are my woman and there's no goddamn reason for him to see you."

"It is his child."

"He's just a sperm donor. I'm that baby's father. He doesn't want kids remember?"

Stephanie nodded solemnly and looked down at her belly again. She was not at all certain that she didn't want to see Todd again. A part of her was curious to see if he would change his mind about kids if he knew that she was carrying his child. Another part of her didn't want to find out the answer.

When the doorbell rang she handed the keys to Cathy, threw herself down onto the couch and covered her head with the pillow.

"It'll be alright, baby. I'll handle it."

Fourteen

"Where's Steph?"

"She doesn't want to see you."

"She didn't say that on the phone."

"She didn't say she wanted to see you, did she? Here's the keys."

Todd took the keys and stared at them.

"Is she still out on a job?"

"A what?"

"She said she had to pick up a bail jumper tonight."

"No, she doesn't do that anymore. I take care of her now."

Cathy was a large woman. At six feet tall she was two inches taller than Todd and she was muscled like a middleweight boxer. She had thighs like a power lifter and Todd wondered what it would feel like to be kicked by legs that muscular. Her foot would probably go right through his chest and explode out of his back. Cathy's bleached blond hair was cut short in a buzz-cut like Annie Lennox. Her breasts were huge, like two large cantaloupes and, unlike Stephanie's, hers appeared to be natural. She was wearing a nine-millimeter Gloch in a shoulder holster and Todd knew that she was into that Ultimate Fighting shit. There were scars on her knuckles and what looked like the faded shadow of a black eye. She had a missing tooth that she'd never bothered to have replaced and a faint scar on her right cheek. She'd probably gotten the black eye fighting with a bail jumper. She was an intimidating woman. Todd could barely make eye contact with her. Cathy would killed him in a fair fight.

"Is she upstairs?"

"Go away, Todd. Make sure you bring the car back before midnight."

Cathy turned her back and shut the door. Todd stood on the porch trying to decide if he should ring the doorbell again. He decided against it.

As he strapped his bike onto the bike rack of Stephanie's Toyota Prius hybrid, Todd could not help but wonder why she'd lied to him about doing a job tonight. Something wasn't right but he didn't have time to think about it for very long. He wondered why she still had the bike rack on the car. Was she still thinking about him? Did she miss him? He needed to move Terrence's body or else he would have stuck around to find out. He'd be back.

Todd started the engine and backed slowly out of the driveway.

He looked up and saw a silhouette in the window staring down at him. He was certain that it was Stephanie. After he was done with Terrence, he had to see her.

Fifteen

The old lady across the street with the house full of cats watched as Todd carried out an armload of plastic wrapped parcels. She'd come out onto the porch when he'd pulled up with Stephanie's car and watched him like a vulture as he unhooked the bike and bike rack and carried them both upstairs. He didn't know what her name was. Todd didn't know any of his neighbors and didn't want to. But he knew her face. It was fat with huge dimpled cheeks, squinty piggish eyes, and a roadmap of wrinkles. The woman was morbidly obese and needed a walker to get around. Her rotund face with the wrinkles and dimples, giving her the look of an ancient cherub, seemed to always be there, peering from beyond the screen door or between her Venetian blinds or, as now, staring blatantly from her front porch.

What the fuck is that old woman doing up so late? Did she stay up just to spy on me?

When he walked upstairs to collect more of Terrence's body parts, she was still sitting on her porch watching him with undisguised curiosity. As he piled the parts into the trunk she craned her neck to get a better look. Cats walked in and out of her house, crowding around her ankles, purring and rubbing up against her. One would disappear back into her house only to be replaced by another.

How many damn cats does that woman have?

By the time he made his last trip up to the apartment to gather up the four individually wrapped quarters of Terrence Mohammed's torso, the woman across the street was on her cell phone and now she was standing up and leaning over her

65

porch railing, petting one of her infinite number of kittens and straining to see what Todd was loading into his trunk. Todd wondered what she thought he was carrying. She probably assumed that they were kilos of coke or meth or marijuana. He wasn't the type of person anyone would have suspected of chopping up a body and stuffing it into a trunk. Unless she'd seen Terrence enter his apartment and not come back out, which was entirely possible. The bitch was always watching.

Todd smiled and waved at her as he hopped into the car. He considered giving her the finger, seriously considered it, but he didn't want to give her anything else to remember about him or piss her off and give her a reason to call the cops if she hadn't already. Todd strapped on his seatbelt and started the engine of Stephanie's black Toyota Prius, wincing as he thought about the carbon footprint he was leaving every time his foot hit the accelerator.

As he turned the corner, Todd realized that he had no idea where he was going.

Where the hell do you go to dump a body?

Todd turned the car toward the Bay. There had to be a deserted section of waterfront where he could toss Terrence's body into the water.

He drove past the souvenir shops, restaurants, boat rentals, the aquarium, and all the other tourist traps, all closed for the night. A policeman on a mountain bike whizzed down the boardwalk as if chasing some unseen suspect. A woman jogged in the opposite direction accompanied by a man on in-line skates. Couples strolled along the waterfront arm-in-arm.

Further down the boardwalk, prostitutes stopped cars in the street and drove off with them to earn their money behind the many warehouses that lined the waterfront. Todd continued to drive until finally he came to an area where there were no more tourists or shops and restaurants or lovers out for moonlit strolls. He stopped in front of an old warehouse with three fishing boats anchored in the water beside it. There were no other buildings for more than a mile except for a condominium project that was still under construction and some sort of shopping mall project that was, so far, no more than a concrete foundation.

Todd drove around to the side of the fish factory and parked next to the trash dumpsters. The smell of dead and decaying fish was overpowering. Todd had to cover his mouth and nose to fend off nausea.

No one's going to notice Terrence with this smell.

The trash dumpsters had locks on them. To keep out pigeons and seagulls, probably. Todd popped the trunk and fished around in the back for the tire iron. It was right underneath Terrence's head. A few swings of the tire iron and the lock gave way. As quickly as he could, Todd began piling the dismembered body parts into the dumpster, burying them deep beneath the rotting fish guts and carcasses.

A huge weight lifted from Todd's shoulders once he'd emptied the car. A big smile of relief spread across Todd's face and he began to hum. It was all over now. Nicolene was taken care of and now so was Terrence. All that remained was for him to return the car to Stephanie and find some way of seeing her.

The drive from the waterfront was long and lonely. The streets were full of late nightclub goers, couples out for a night of dinner and dancing, friends bar-hopping, and singles on the prowl for a bed-mate for the evening. Todd felt disconnected from all of them. He could not understand why anyone would drive a car. He felt alienated enough from humanity without this extra barrier between them. At least if he was walking or riding his bike he could pretend that he was somehow a part of the festivities. Now, riding by watching it through the car window, he felt completely alone.

When Todd turned off the main streets into the more residential neighborhoods, it was as if the world was suddenly deserted. Despite the streetlights, the blocks seemed darker without the neon signs from the bars and storefronts. The sidewalks were empty and the houses were dark except for the flickering blue light from the occasional television shining from a living room or bedroom window or a kitchen light left on in anticipation of a midnight snack. Surprisingly, Todd felt less alone here than he had on Market Street.

Todd pulled up in front of Stephanie's apartment building. All the lights were on in her apartment. The shades had not been drawn and he could see right into her living room. Stephanie and Cathy were sitting on the couch watching a movie. Todd parked across the street so he could watch for a moment before they noticed he'd arrived. He killed the engine and sat there for a while. Stephanie's face looked rounder than he remembered it and even sitting down he could tell that her breasts had gotten bigger. Had she increased the size of her implants?

Other than that, she looked exactly the same. It had only been five months since he'd seen her last so he hadn't really expected her to change much. Part of him was expecting her to have become some butch lesbian with a mullet and a flannel shirt. She was living up to one stereotype though. She had definitely gained weight. Todd stepped out of the car and walked across the street. He stood outside of Stephanie's apartment, not knocking or ringing the doorbell, just staring through the window. Stephanie had gained even more weight than he'd thought. They were eating popcorn and she had the popcorn bowl sitting on top of an enormous belly. Suddenly, she stood up and walked to the kitchen. A chill raced down his spine and he cried out. Stephanie turned toward the window and she saw him just as he saw her...all of her. Stephanie was pregnant.

She gasped and covered her mouth. Cathy bolted from the couch and ran to the window. Todd just stood there, staring.

Seconds later the front door opened and Cathy walked out looking pissed. Stephanie was behind her. Todd just stared at her with his mouth still hanging open.

"I wanted to tell you." Her eyes were full of tears. So were Todd's.

"You don't have to say shit to him. What the fuck are you doing peepin' in our windows?" Cathy pushed him and Todd fell down hard on his ass. He was still just staring at Stephanie's belly with his mouth hanging open. Mute.

Stephanie grabbed Cathy and pulled her away from Todd just as the big woman was balling up her fists looking like she was preparing to pound Todd into the concrete.

"Let me talk to him. Just go in the house. I'll be in, in a minute. Just let me talk to him."

Cathy looked worried, angry, but she turned slowly, still glaring murderously at Todd, and walked back into the apartment.

Stephanie held out a hand for Todd. Todd just stared at it and then back at her stomach.

"I'm pregnant, Todd. Nine months pregnant. I was pregnant the night we broke up. It's your baby."

Todd shook his head slowly as the tears began to race down his face. He looked down at his messenger bag. The stun gun was still in there and so was the scalpel and the clamps and the cat gut. He was out of duct tape but he still had the handcuffs.

"It's your baby. You're going to be a father whether you like it or not." Stephanie was crying too but her voice was strong and she stuck out her jaw defiantly while at the same time searching Todd's face for some sign of joy, some indication that he might have been pleased by the idea of parenthood. What she saw instead was terror and anger and sadness.

Todd stood up and reached out for her belly. She let him touch it, still watching his expression, hoping it would change. His hands trembled as he touched Stephanie's stomach. He rubbed his palms over it, thinking about the fetus he'd ripped out of Nicolene and strangled with its own umbilical cord, wondering if he could do that to his own child. He balled up his fists and Stephanie flinched and pulled away from him. He looked up into her eyes, brow furrowed, nose wrinkled, lip pulled up into a scowl, jaw tight, teeth gritting together, fists still clenched. The look on his face told Stephanie everything without saying a word.

How could you?

He reached into his bag and Stephanie took two more steps back. He grabbed the stun gun and gripped it tight. Then he let it go. He fished around some more until he found the scalpel. He thought about punching the knife into her gut and carving the baby out of her right there in front of her apartment. But he couldn't. He loved Stephanie. He looked down at her belly. He didn't know what to do.

His hand was still in the bag, still gripping the scalpel. His face was a riot of ticks and twitches as he sobbed louder, his entire body hitching and jerking as the force of his tears racked his body. He he was in agony. Stephanie took a step toward him. He stepped back and his face twisted into a scowl then he began to laugh. His laughter rose louder and louder. It was the sound of a mind that had lost all connection with sanity. Tears continued to rain from his eyes as he doubled over with laughter. He turned abruptly and walked off down the street, still laughing. The absurd irony of Stephanie carrying his baby while he was on a campaign to stop everyone in the world from having more kids was just further proof that no one had a more fucked up sense of humor than God. Todd had gotten his vasectomy too late.

Todd could feel Stephanie's eyes on his back, watching him walk off into the night. He could hear her painful sobs. He heard the door to their apartment open and Cathy storm out.

"It's your baby, Todd! It's your baby!" Stephanie's voice sounded hysterical. He had hurt her. It was the last thing he'd wanted to do when he'd decided to call her, the last thing he'd wanted to do when he'd pulled up in front of her apartment just minutes ago. But everything had gone wrong. She was pregnant.

Todd wanted to go back. He wanted to hug her and tell her that everything would be alright, that they would raise the baby together, and that they would be a family. But he didn't because he knew that if he went back there…he would kill her.

"Fuck you, Todd! You'd better never come back here again! I'd better never see you again, do you hear me?" It was Cathy and he knew she meant it. She'd try to kill him if he came back again. Unless he killed her first.

Sixteen

Work the next morning was surreal. The night before he'd been cutting open a young crackwhore and disposing of a man's body and today he was listening to an elderly woman talk to him about how Medicare wasn't covering her bills and she needed food stamps.

"I'm sorry but you can't be on both Medicare and food stamps." The woman looked impossibly ancient. Her body was thin and drawn and her skin was a maze of fissures and wrinkles. Her hair was completely white and her eyes looked yellow and rheumy. Her left eye was white with cataracts.

"Well, what am I supposed to do? I can't afford my medications and keep the heat on and buy food."

"I'm sorry but I can't help you."

Todd was exhausted and his head was pounding. He looked beyond the old woman at the endless line of applicants and then at the front door of the building, wondering if the police were going to burst in any minute and arrest him for what he'd done to Nicolene or for killing Terrence but there were just more welfare applicants streaming into the building in an endless tide.

I've got to get the hell out of here!

"I'm sorry but we're done here. I've got a lot of other people to see and I'm not feeling well."

He rose and walked out of his cubicle just as his supervisor was preparing to walk in.

"The cops are here. It seems they had a complaint about you from some junkie whore. She says that you stole her baby."

71

The woman seemed amused by it. As if she was enjoying the drama. Todd followed her back to her office.

They walked past all of the fat and morbidly obese people waiting in line for food stamps, the young able-bodied men and women lined up to apply for welfare checks when they ought to have been applying for jobs, the pregnant women on their third, fourth, or fifth child, standing in line for WIC food vouchers, the gangbangers, pimps, and drug dealers waiting by the front door for their whores to get their checks and bring them the money. Todd asked himself if what he had done was wrong and he just couldn't see it. He couldn't see how anyone could have blamed him. Even if they didn't know what we were doing to the environment, this should have been enough to convince them. Scum like this should not be allowed to reproduce.

The cops stood in front of Ms. Santiago's desk looking bored and annoyed. One of the cops approached Todd as they entered. He was about 5'9" and over two hundred pounds. Body by Big Mac. His gut hung over his belt, hiding the buckle. He didn't appear to be much older than thirty and looked Native American. His partner was a skinny white guy who looked like he was in his forties. They both shook Todd's hand and smiled insincerely. Todd returned the smile.

"Todd Hammerstein, right?"

"Yes?"

"We've just got a few questions for you about a young woman named Nicolene De Marco."

"The name sounds familiar. Who is she?"

The two cops studied Todd's face, looking for the lie.

"She came in with her husband a few days ago trying to get on public assistance. You took her application."

"Oh, that's probably why her name sounds familiar. Is she wanted for something? If she just came in I should still have her application. I can probably get her address for you."

"No, we know where she is. She's in the hospital. She claims that someone gave her an abortion against her will. She was six months pregnant at the time. It looks like they cut her baby right out of the womb."

Todd turned white and began to look ill, as he remembered what he'd done.

"That's horrible!"

Todd looked over at his boss. She was still smirking.

"She thinks that you may have had something to do with it Mr. Hammerstein."

"Me?"

"She says that you tried to talk her into having an abortion and getting her tubes tied. Kind of a coincidence since that's exactly what happened to her. Are you okay Mr. Hammerstein?"

"Not really. I was about to go home sick. I've been getting really bad headaches lately. Migraines."

"Well, we won't keep you very long. What about what Mrs. De Marco said?"

"Who?"

"Mrs. De Marco. The woman who was assaulted? Did you try to convince her to have an abortion?"

"That's not really what we do here. We don't have time for that kind of counseling. We just assess need and accept or decline the applications. We get so many applicants that we just don't have much time to spend with each one."

"I told him the same thing," Ms. Santiago said. "So then why would she say that?"

The police officer with the big gut turned to Todd's supervisor, still looking annoyed.

"Are you serious? We hear all kinds of bullshit in here. Probably as much as you get in your job, officer. Saying that the government wants poor people to have abortions isn't really a new one. We hear that every day around here. Probably as often as you hear about racist cops targeting minorities."

The cops nodded their heads, smiling as if to say "touché'" and then turned back to Todd. Todd's eyes were closed and he was swaying back and forth, rubbing his temples with his index fingers. His head felt like it was being slowly peeled open like a hard-boiled egg.

"You really don't look so good, buddy. How about you come down to the station tomorrow when you're feeling better and we can talk about this some more then?"

Todd nodded his head.

They shook hands again and one of the cops, officer Dickerson, handed Todd his card. After they left, Todd's supervisor was still standing there staring at him.

"Sit down, Todd."

Todd took a seat in front of her desk. Unlike the cheap plastic seats the applicants sat in his cubicle, these chairs were made out of metal and vinyl and swiveled.

"I covered for you just now. The only complaints we've ever gotten about anyone trying to convince an applicant to have an abortion were about you, the other day, with that Black lady. Now, I hope we don't have a problem here?"

"There's no problem, Ms. Santiago."

"And you didn't have anything to do with that woman getting cut open?"

"I'd have to be crazy to do something like that."

"That's not exactly a no."

She stared directly into Todd's eyes, still smirking, still amused by all of this.

"No. I had nothing to do with it."

"Good. Go home, Todd. Get some rest. I'll see you tomorrow after your meeting with the cops."

Todd nodded his head and turned to leave.

"You know, there's a shelter for unwed mothers over on D Street."

"A what?"

"It's run by one of those Right to Life groups. They talk pregnant girls into keeping their babies and not having abortions and in exchange they give them free room and board during and after their pregnancies and then help them find couples to adopt their babies. You could always tell your clients to go there if they won't get an abortion. I mean, between you and me, I agree with you. They shouldn't be having all of these damned kids that they can't even take care of. There are already too many people in the world without us cluttering up the planet even more with all of these unwanted kids."

Todd said nothing. He just stared at her, trying to read her, trying to figure her out.

Why the hell did she just tell me all of that?

She winked at him and shrugged her shoulders. "Just an FYI." Todd turned and walked out of her office.

Seventeen

Todd had walked to work. After the night he'd had, he needed to clear his head. Walking gave him an opportunity to think and clear his head. As Todd walked out of the Department of Welfare, he was thinking about Stephanie and his child. Leaving the baby alive made him feel like a hypocrite. How could he take Nicolene's baby for the good of the planet but make his own child some sort of exception? It wasn't right. But how could he abort his own child?

This was all Stephanie's fault. He'd never wanted children. She'd known that all along and yet she'd allowed herself to get pregnant anyway. He could have used a condom, of course, but she'd said that she was on the pill. He had trusted her and she'd betrayed him. She was every bit as guilty as Nicolene. But there was no way he could cut her open the way he'd done that crackwhore. He loved her. Besides, Cathy would have broken both of his legs and shot his testicles off before he could have gotten close to Stephanie.

Unless I can get to Cathy first. If I can surprise her and hit her with the stun gun I should be able to handcuff and gag her before she can shoot me or kick my ass or something. If I can do it quietly I should be able to get Stephanie before she can run. Or maybe I can get Stephanie while Cathy is out chasing bail jumpers?

Todd considered how much energy he was putting into planning something he had told himself he wouldn't do. He reached into his messenger bag and grabbed the scalpel. He slid his thumb over the blade and drew blood. The pain helped him to organize his thoughts.

She has to die.

It was simple and direct. He couldn't murder their child and look Stephanie in the face ever again. It would be easier if both child and mom were gone.

And Cathy too.

If he didn't kill her she'd hunt him to the ends of the earth. Todd walked to the hardware store around the corner.

"Still heading up to Mammoth Mountain? I heard there might be rain up there."

"What?"

"You bought an axe the other day for your camping trip at Mammoth Mountain. I thought you might of put it off."

"I'm still going. I need to pick up a few more things."

Todd picked up another four pack of duct tape and threw it into his shopping basket. As an afterthought, he grabbed a claw hammer and threw that in as well.

"Doing repairs on the cabin," Todd offered before the old store clerk could comment. He paid quickly and left.

Todd made one more stop on the way home. He went into the medical supply store and bought a pack of disposable scalpels. He walked home slowly and changed his mind several times before he reached his apartment. Each time he began to doubt his course he ran his thumb along the scalpel blade and remembered the baby he'd strangled with the umbilical cord in the name of the environment. That memory kept him on course. If he didn't get rid of Stephanie's baby then his entire mission was a lie and he was little more than a murderer. He went upstairs to his apartment and got his bike. He needed to do it before he lost his nerve and changed his mind.

He pedaled hard, dodging between cars and hopping curbs as if he was being chased. He thought about Heimlich's plan to put Progesterex into the drinking water of the 25 most populated cities in the world. It was so much better than what he was doing. What he was doing would barely change anything. He had saved perhaps a couple hundred animals and maybe as many trees and plants. Nothing in the grand scheme of things. He could only hope that he would become a symbol of some sort, like Heimlich, an example for others to follow.

Todd arrived in Stephanie's neighborhood, sweaty and exhausted. Her car was still in its parking space but she could have been in Cathy's car. He had no idea what Cathy drove. He imagined her to be the type to drive a Harley Davidson, the kind with the handlebars that stuck up as high as your head. Todd cruised slowly by the window of her apartment and peeked in. The vertical blinds were partially closed but he could still see in-between them. He saw Stephanie sitting on the couch, staring at the TV screen. She was still so beautiful, even with the added weight of pregnancy. She stood up and walked into the kitchen. Todd pedaled away before she could spot him. He needed to find a place where he could watch from a distance. Once Cathy left the apartment he could sneak inside and do what needed to be done.

There was an old house across the street sitting on a quarter of an acre of overgrown vegetation. It didn't look like anyone lived there. Todd parked his bike in a copse of trees on the edge of the property and took his place among the oversized shrubs and hedges and waited, fingering the scalpel in his messenger bag.

Eighteen

Stephanie had still not recovered from her meeting with Todd the night before. She sat on the couch watching one soap opera after another and eating Ben and Jerry's ice cream. It surprised her how much seeing Todd had affected her. It was obvious that she still had unresolved feelings for him. He was her baby's father. It was obvious to Cathy too. Even as Cathy had tried to console her after Todd had left, she could see the wounded look on the woman's face.

Stephanie loved Cathy. But she wasn't in love with her. If Todd had changed his mind about the baby and asked her to marry him and raise their child together, she would have left Cathy in a heartbeat. As much as she tried to keep those emotions to herself, she was afraid that Cathy knew it. Stephanie knew that Cathy would do anything for her. The woman was fiercely protective. She also had a bit of a temper and Stephanie was more than a little afraid of her. She had never been afraid of Todd.

Todd had been a welcome break from the muscle-bound pretty boys she usually dated. Men who had cheated on her and beaten her, used her, and abandoned her. Men who degraded her and took all of her money. Todd had been gentle and caring. He had bought her things and complimented her constantly. He was always telling her how beautiful she was. She used to catch him staring at her out of the corner of her eye as if he was completely in awe of her. She knew that Todd had been a virgin when they met. That had only endeared him to her more. He was so sweet and innocent and he looked at her as if she was some sort of angel.

He didn't know about how she'd run away from home at fifteen to follow her favorite rock band around the country. How she'd wound up sneaking backstage to meet the band. She'd been excited when the lead guitarist had invited her back to their hotel room and flattered when he and the lead singer had begun kissing and undressing her. Then the drummer and the bass player had come in along with their entire entourage and the night had ended with her getting gangbanged by the band and then passed around among the band's roadies and hangers on before being kicked out of the hotel room at four o'clock in the morning, her face, thighs, and stomach still tacky with semen from more than a dozen different men. She'd spent the next year selling herself on the street before moving in with a guy who had seemed like her savior before he'd begun beating her every day. Todd didn't know how she'd finally stabbed him and then fled after he'd nearly beaten her to death.

All Todd knew was how she'd gone back to college and gotten her Bachelors degree after being homeless for three years. Todd knew her as a fighter and he respected her. She knew that he suspected she'd been through a lot but he'd never asked for details. He'd let her deal with her demons her own way. When she'd decided that she wanted to be a bounty hunter he'd been concerned but supportive. He knew that she had needed something to make her feel empowered and if tackling criminals was what it took then he was okay with that. He loved her. But he had looked disgusted, disappointed, and enraged when he had seen that she was pregnant with his child. He had rejected her just like every other man she'd ever gotten involved with from her workaholic daddy on down. Cathy would never reject her.

Stephanie pulled herself out of the chair and waddled into the kitchen. Her stomach was so big she felt like she was having twins. She put the ice cream back into the freezer and started making herself a cup of coffee. She needed to get herself going. She couldn't just lay on the couch eating ice cream all day and feeling sorry for herself. That would have been too typical. A walk would do her some good. She'd already gained more than the recommended amount of baby weight. If she didn't want to still weigh two hundred pounds after the baby was born she knew she needed to keep exercising. There was a park just a few blocks away with a track, a family park where new mothers pushed their strollers along a tree-lined path and other pregnant women power-walked in a desperate bid to preserve what they could of their figures from the inevitable pregnancy weight gain.

As she waited for her coffee, she rubbed a combination of vitamin E and cocoa butter on her stomach, hips, ass and thighs. Her OBGYN had said that stretch marks had more to do with genetics than moisturizers but she figured that it couldn't hurt. Cathy hadn't gotten up yet. She'd stayed up with Stephanie until four in the morning, holding her while she cried uncontrollably. Then she tucked Stephanie into bed and went out to catch the child molester who'd missed his court date the previous week. Cathy was a good woman and Stephanie knew she was lucky to have her, even if the woman did frighten her sometimes.

The coffee pot boiled and Stephanie poured herself a cup. She found herself repeatedly looking out the window as she sipped her coffee, hoping still that Todd would change his mind and do the right thing. But every time she allowed herself to fantasize about what life would be like for her and Todd raising a little boy or girl together, she remembered that look on his face, his tears that had erupted violently and then turned to that insane laughter. He looked like he had lost his mind. When he had reached into his bag she'd had a moment where she'd been afraid he was going to pull out a gun or a knife. It was the first and only time she'd ever been afraid of Todd.

Stephanie finished her coffee, changed into a pair of sweatpants and a t-shirt, put on a pair of running shoes and headed out the door. She strapped her iPod to her arm and put her headphones on. Stephanie fast-forwarded through Madonna and Alanis Morissette, Mariah Carey and Metallica until she found a Whitney Houston song that fit her mood. She power-walked down the sidewalk singing out loud.

"It's not right. But it's okaaay. I'm gonna make it anyway. Pack your bags. Up and leave. Don't you dare come running back to meeeee." She smiled as she imagined herself saying those words to Todd.

After only five minutes of walking Stephanie began to sweat and breathe heavily.

Jesus, I'm out of shape! she thought.

By the time she reached the park she had to rest on a bench to catch her breath. She watched the mothers and babysitters strolling along the jogging path, gossiping and laughing to one another. A man pushing a jogging-stroller sprinted past along with three other men. A large woman in her early forties power-walked with a small Dachshund yapping at her heels. Bikers, skateboarders, and rollerbladers raced by, ignoring the signs posted everywhere warning that the path was for joggers and walkers only.

After about three minutes, Stephanie struggled to her feet and fell in step behind the woman with the Dachshund. The woman's pace was a bit slower than the pace Stephanie had kept on her way to the park which suited Stephanie just fine. She wanted to walk for at least twenty minutes and there was no way she could have done that speed-walking.

She'd gone two laps around the quarter-mile track and was lost in an Alanis Morissette song about falling head over feet for some guy. Her head was down, staring at the track. She was still thinking about Todd. When she looked up she thought she saw Todd riding a bike right at her. The closer the bike came the more the rider resembled Todd. When he was just ten yards away and she could see the tears racing down his face, she was certain that it was Todd. He'd come back to her. She stopped and took off her headphones. She smiled and tears welled up in her eyes. Todd kept coming. His bike never slowed. His hand reached into his messenger bag and this time Stephanie was expecting him to pull out a bouquet of roses or, better yet, an engagement ring. When she saw the hammer in his hand a look of confusion crossed her face. She was still wondering what the hammer was for when he buried it in her stomach, doubling her over.

Stephanie dropped to her knees, writhing in agony and vomiting uncontrollably while trying to catch her breath at the same time. Her guts were on fire. She looked up at Todd as he walked over to her, still carrying the hammer. He was sobbing and shaking his head as if trying to deny some unspoken truth.

81

"I'm sorry, Stephanie. I'm so sorry."

She tried to get to her feet and instead rolled over onto her back, reeling in pain and holding her belly. Todd brought the hammer down again. And it felt as if the baby inside of her collapsed beneath the blow. Her belly seemed to deflate a little and blood stained the crotch of her sweatpants.

"I love you, Stephanie."

He brought the hammer down again and again. Stephanie never even screamed. She moaned and whimpered but she never screamed. Her mouth filled with blood that exploded out onto the jogging path as he struck her again.

Stephanie never heard his declaration of love. The pain was so huge that it blotted out the entire world. Her only thought was that her baby was dead. She had a dead baby inside of her. Her next thought was worry for Todd. Cathy was going to kill him for this.

Nineteen

Todd could not think straight. He pedaled as fast as he could. His eyesight was obscured by tears. He had no idea where he was going or if he was being pursued.

I killed Stephanie.

The words were unbelievable to him. He couldn't reconcile the person he knew himself to be with what he knew he had done. He wasn't a murderer. He loved everyone. He only wanted to save the planet, save everyone from extinction. How could he have murdered two people and vivisected another? This had to be some kind of nightmare.

But hadn't I always said that if taking one human life or even a hundred would save millions for countless generations than it was a moral duty to take those lives? Hadn't I said that?

Heimlich had said that. Those were his words, from his book. And now Heimlich was behind bars, probably for the rest of his life, for trying to sterilize hundreds of millions of women. And Todd would probably get locked up too for what he'd done to Nicolene and Terrence and now Stephanie.

I killed her. I killed Stephanie.

Todd had been conflicted right up until the moment he'd swung the hammer into her pregnant belly, pulverizing their unborn child. He wasn't positive that he'd killed Stephanie. He had intended to crack her skull with the hammer to finish her off but he'd hesitated. There had been a tenderness in her eyes, a sadness and a sympathy and it had been for him. She'd felt sympathy for him as he was standing above her after repeatedly bludgeoning her stomach with a hammer, preparing to split her skull open with the next blow. She'd looked confused and frightened but still in love, still in love with him. He supposed that it was some perverse version of battered women's syndrome. She had been abused before. Perhaps, somewhere deep inside her, she equated abuse with love. He didn't know—wasn't sure—didn't want to psychoanalyze it. All he knew was that she hadn't hated him, even as he was preparing to beat her to death, she hadn't hated him. And so he had hesitated.

A group of men, who'd also been jogging on the path, came charging toward him. One of them was pushing a stroller. Todd had a moment to register the absurdity of someone pushing a baby stroller toward a guy who'd just bludgeoned a pregnant woman with a hammer before he picked up his bike and pedaled out of the park as fast as he could.

He didn't know if Stephanie was dead but he was pretty damned sure she wouldn't be having any babies.

Todd didn't know where to go now. He didn't know what to do. The police would be looking for him now. His mission would be over soon and he'd done so little. Heimlich was about to sterilize an entire city and all he'd done was talk an overweight trailer park welfare queen into getting rid of her baby, murder a womanizing insemination machine, sterilize a crackwhore and abort her baby, and now murdered his own unborn child. It didn't seem like nearly enough. He hadn't continued Heimlich's work. He hadn't made a difference. He needed to do more. Before the cops caught up with him, he needed to make a real impact. He'd probably murdered Stephanie for the cause. He couldn't stop now.

He rode down to Market Street, tossed his bike into an alley and caught a bus uptown. His heart was beating as if it was trying to pound its way through his rib cage. He must have looked like a criminal, looking over his shoulder and slouching down whenever a patrol car passed. He was just about to exit the bus when an advertisement caught his eye.

It said, "Life begins at conception. Let us help you save a life." It was an ad for a place called Haven House, a shelter for unwed mothers. This was the place his supervisor had told him about. Todd walked to the front of the bus. He leaned down and spoke to the bus driver.

"How do I get to D Street and Fifth Avenue?"

"Get off here and catch the westbound subway. Get off at the Fifth Avenue station."

"Thank You."

Todd left the bus and headed to the subway. He still had his messenger bag full of medical supplies and hand tools. There was still more good that he could do.

On the subway, Todd stared openly at a young couple, teenagers, obviously in love. They hugged and kissed each other with a tenderness that only came from hard times and a relationship too new to have become accustomed to grief and strife. Todd wanted to tell them never to have kids. He wanted to make them understand.

"Hey."

Todd leaned over and whispered to the couple that who were practically spooning in the subway seat. They didn't look at him or even appear to notice that he had spoken.

"Hey!" Todd said a bit louder. This time they both turned and looked at him. The woman looked annoyed but the guy, who looked like some hybrid of a grunge rocker and a hippy, smiled pleasantly as if awakening from a beautiful dream. He even blinked and yawned.

"What's up, man?"

"You two are in love, huh?"

This time they both smiled. The girl was just a tad overweight with tiny breasts and wide hips. She was dressed in all black with black lipstick, eye-shadow, and blood red fingernail polish. Her hair was dyed completely white. She'd probably spent many a lonely night reading Ann Sexton and Emily Dickenson while listening to The Cure and Depeche Mode, or whoever their current day equivalents were, before she'd met the man of her dreams. They both looked like they'd once kept lists of schoolmates they wanted to murder.

"Yeah, we're in love."

"I love him."

"Don't have kids. You can get married and love each other forever, but never have kids. Adopt kids. There're plenty of kids out there that need parents without adding to the backlog. But this world is already overpopulated. In your lifetime the world's population will double. Just think about that. For every asshole, every criminal, every annoying bothersome pest, in about sixty years, there will be two of them."

The two lovers sat there with their smiles falling and rising as they tried to figure out if he was serious.

"Man, you are crazy as hell!" the boy declared, laughing, slapping his knee, and shaking his head. He looked at his girlfriend but her face was dead serious.

"He's right though. It's just like that guy on TV, the one who tried to poison the water in New York. He said the same thing. We're like a cancer growing out of control, killing the planet. But what should we do?"

"Get yourselves fixed. Sterilize yourselves."

"But what about everyone else? What do we do about all the other breeders?" the boy said, still giggling, taking the entire thing as some sort of joke.

The subway pulled into the station at 5th Avenue. Todd rose to leave. The two teens were still looking at him, waiting for a reply, waiting for him to speak some profound words of wisdom.

"Sterilize them too."

He stepped out of the subway and the doors swished closed behind him. The young couple was still staring at him as the subway raced past. It was time to make a difference.

It didn't take him long to locate the women's shelter. It was an old red brick Victorian with a big wooden sign that said "Haven House" hanging from the porch roof above the steps to the front door.

Todd didn't know anything about the women's shelter except that its owners were the type who'd bombed abortion clinics in the eighties and stood outside of women's clinics with posters of aborted fetuses. The only reason the shelter existed was to convince women who would have otherwise aborted their babies to carry them to term. This place was the negation of everything Todd stood for. Todd pulled the hammer and the stun gun out of the messenger bag and rang the doorbell.

A woman in her sixties opened the door. She had deep crow's feet in the corners of her eyes, flabby jowls that hung down past her jaw like a Bassett hound, turkey-like waddle

86

hanging from her neck and breasts that looked far too perky for a woman her age, an obvious boob job. When she smiled her teeth were far too-white caps, dental implants, or dentures, but definitely not her own teeth. She was the very picture of a woman struggling desperately to hang on to the last vestiges of youth. Todd didn't bother to return her smile. Instead he zapped her with the stun gun and clubbed her over the head with the hammer. He felt the resistance of her skull and then felt it give with a wet crack.

Her legs folded under her as she collapsed like an imploding building, tumbling straight down and whacking her already bloody skull on the hardwood floor with a loud *Thwap!* Blood gushed from the wound and stained the floor. She didn't appear to be breathing. She was probably the owner of the place so, in Todd's mind, she'd gotten what she deserved. Her death would hopefully prevent any other young girls from having babies they didn't want and that the world didn't need. He stepped over her and walked into the house, kicking the door shut behind him and then locking it.

Twenty

There was a woman lying on the living room couch watching television. She barely looked up when Todd entered the room.

"Who was it at the door?"

"Me," Todd answered as he walked up behind her and clamped a hand over her mouth. He zapped her and taped her up before she could make a noise.

An old man who was probably the husband of the woman he'd cracked at the front door, was sitting in the den typing away on a laptop when Todd stormed into the room. The old guy jumped and almost fell out of his chair.

"Jesus! Who the fuck are you?"

"I'm sort of a Pro-Life activist also."

The old guy squinted, trying to see Todd standing in the darkened doorway. He fumbled for his glasses on his cluttered desk.

"What organization are you with?"

Todd stepped further into the room.

"Mass-Murderers for the Preservation of Animal Life."

The old guy found his glasses and slipped them onto his crinkled, liver-spotted scalp.

"Mass-Murderers? Wha-What?"

Todd stepped closer and the old guy flicked on his desktop lamp and turned it up so that it shone directly onto Todd's face.

The old guy looked Todd up and down, noting the bloody hammer still clutched in Todd's hand and the stun gun clasped in his other hand. He reached into his desk and Todd sprinted across the room and cracked him with the hammer before he could pull the .357 Colt magnum revolver out of his top drawer. The gun tumbled to the floor and so did the old man. Todd tried not to look at the old guy bleeding on the floor as he reached into his bag and retrieved the duct tape.

Though the man looked nothing like either his father or the priest, the old guy was probably twenty years older than his father had been when he'd taken his own life, something about the scene reminded him of the night of his mother's funeral. The night Todd lost both of his parents.

The old man moaned and struggled meekly as Todd taped his arms behind his back and put tape on his eyes and mouth. Todd picked up the gun, checked the barrel, then clicked it back into place and cocked the hammer. He left the room and headed back out into the hallway. There were voices coming from the kitchen. Todd walked into the kitchen and pointed the gun from one face to the other. He was greeted with a chorus of screams. There were several women sitting at the small kitchen table sipping coffee and eating some kind of coffee cakes. They jumped up quickly, knocking over chairs and dropping cups to the floor.

"Shut the fuck up and sit back down. One more sound and I will kill every last one of you."

Todd tossed a roll of tape to a teenage girl wearing a ponytail who was just starting to show. She looked to be about three or four months pregnant. There were four other women, two more that appeared to be in their early teens, a black woman in her thirties and a Filipino woman in her early to mid-twenties. They were all in varying stages of pregnancy.

"Tape their hands behind their backs or I start shooting."

Three more women came rushing into the kitchen and Todd turned the gun toward them. A huge white woman with curlers in her hair, a robe that barely concealed her massive belly and gigantic breasts that each appeared to weigh as much as small Thanksgiving turkeys, shrieked like a cat in a microwave when she spotted the gun. Todd cracked the butt of the revolver across her lips. Teeth flew from her mouth against the wall and she staggered backwards almost knocking over the other two women. Todd noted with surprise that the voice he normally heard in his head, the one that was always questioning his actions, telling him that

89

he was going too far, begging him to stop, was silent. Even when the woman dropped slowly to her knees, sobbing and holding her bleeding mouth, Todd felt nothing at all.

"Get over there with the rest of them." He gestured with the gun toward the women sitting at the table and the three new arrivals shuffled over there hugging each other. Todd tossed the other three rolls of tape to the three girls.

"Tape up the rest of them."

He pointed at the teenage girl he'd singled out earlier.

"I'll tape you up myself. You make sure everyone else is bound nice and tight. Don't think you're doing anyone any favors by not taping them up good. I'll be checking everyone's wrists and ankles when you're done. If anyone gets free I'm shooting them dead as an example to everyone else."

"Don't kill us, Mister. We're pregnant. We're all pregnant. This is a shelter for pregnant women."

"I know exactly what this place is." There was no expression on his face at all as he pointed the gun at the girls.

"We don't have any money."

"I don't want any."

"Well, we-we'll do whatever you want. Just don't kill us. Don't hurt us."

"I don't want to fuck you either. Now everybody stop talking. Tape their mouths closed."

The three girls finished taping up the other four girls and then one by one the teenage girl with the ponytail taped them up as well. After she'd put the gags on their mouths she turned to face Todd.

"Please don't hurt me."

"Turn around."

She did as she was told and Todd taped her wrists behind her back like the seven other women.

"Sit in the chair."

"Please, don't."

"I told you. I'm not going to kill you."

She sat down and Todd taped her ankles to the chair legs. He pulled off another strip of tape and placed it over her eyes.

"Are there any more women in the house? Anyone else here I should know about?"

The girl shook her head.

"I don't like surprises. If anyone surprises me you'll all die." Todd ripped off another piece of tape.

"My name is Mary. I'm having a daughter. Her name is going to be Kelli."

Todd paused. He knew what she was doing. Trying to make herself real to him, to make herself more of a human being. She thought that would make it harder for him to kill her. Todd waited, expecting the sting of conscience to hit him.

"My daughter's name is going to be Kelli. She's my second child. My other daughter is Cindy. She's two years old. Her birthday was last week."

He felt nothing. Killing his own child had taken away the last vestiges of his humanity. Todd put the tape over her mouth. He leaned forward and whispered into Mary's ear.

"You're going to have to give all your love to the child you have now."

He rubbed her belly with the palm of his hand. "This one ain't going to make it."

Todd reached into his bag and pulled out a scalpel and a wire hanger. He knelt down beside Mary and began cutting off her pajamas. He cut up the inside of her pants leg all the way to her crotch and down the opposite leg.

"This is really going to hurt but it will be worth it. You are going to save so many people and thousands of plants and animals just by not having this child."

After straightening the hanger out until it was just a long thin wire with a hook on the end of it, Todd parted her labia with his thumb and index fingers and began winding the hanger up inside of her. The blood came almost immediately.

Mommy bled too. Mommy bled because we couldn't afford another child. Mommy bled because the child wasn't daddy's.

Todd remembered that tiny head with the wire hanger poked through the eye socket being dragged out of his mother's hairy snatch. He shoved the hanger in deeper and the girl jerked and bucked screaming against the tape over her mouth. Rocking back and forth against the chair back and almost toppling the chair onto the floor.

"This is the best way. This is how my mommy did it. But if you don't stay still and let me get this parasite out of you, I'm going to have to cut it right out of your uterus."

The girl's legs shook. Her body trembled. But she didn't try to knock the chair over again.

Blood poured from the young woman's vagina. As Todd began driving the hanger in and out of her with greater and greater force the woman began to jerk back and forth and slam herself against the back of her chair. The blood continued to flow out of her but now some of the blood was chunky. Bloody globs dripped from her snatch and plopped onto the floor. It looked like chili meat, like chunks of carne asada in a red enchilada sauce. Todd's stomach was calm this time as he continued to plunge her vagina with the hanger, removing bits of fetal tissue that looked like beef stew. Even after he had removed the hanger, blood and pulp continued to drip from her vagina onto the floor.

Todd grabbed the big woman with the generous breasts and put the gun to her temple. She was further along than all the other women. She looked as if she was ready to give birth at any second. Todd didn't think he was going to need the hanger for her.

He flipped her bathrobe up over her head revealing her naked ass then bent her over the kitchen sink. He pushed the barrel of the revolver into her right cheek.

"You fucking move. You fucking die. Do you understand?"

He reached into a rack on the side of the sink and pulled out a steak knife. He knelt down and sawed in half the tape securing her ankles together. Then he pulled a pair of rubber gloves out of his messenger bag and slipped them onto his hands. He used what looked like fried chicken grease from a pot that was sitting in the sink to lube up his fingers.

Todd kept the gun pressed into the big woman's cheek as he eased one finger then two then three then his entire hand into her vagina. She screamed and wept and moaned and cursed as Todd pushed his hand deeper inside of her. She bled profusely, as Todd's arm disappeared inside her up to the elbow. Todd pushed his fingers through the woman's cervix until he felt what he thought was the baby's head. He seized it and pulled.

Something squirmed in his hands. The big woman was sweating and screaming and shaking as Todd slowly dragged a nearly fully developed fetus from her womb. Her vagina split and tore as the baby's head emerged in a gush of blood and amniotic fluid that pooled on the floor between her feet. Her legs buckled and she started to fall.

"If you drop, you'll land on your baby and kill it. Then I'll kill you."

The woman straightened her legs and held herself up. Todd grabbed the baby's head with both hands now and jerked hard as if he was trying to decapitate the infant while it was still inside its mother. The baby spilled out of the woman and fell to the floor, still attached to its mother. Todd thought about how he'd killed his own baby. If he could do that to his own child, if his mother could kill his brother in the womb, he couldn't show mercy to anyone else's child. Todd raised his shoe and stomped down on the baby's head, rupturing it like a rotten cantaloupe and squirting blood and brain matter out of its ears. He threw the child's mother to the floor with the umbilical cord still trailing out of her vagina attached to her murdered child. The woman fell beside her child, hitting the floor face first into her child's brain tissue and blood mixed with her own blood and fluids. Todd turned to the rest of the women and picked up the hanger again.

He pulled three more of the mothers-to-be from where they huddled in the corner of the room and pushed them down into the three remaining kitchen chairs, releasing their ankles and securing them instead to the chair legs. He then cut off their sweatpants, pajama pants, and panties. The first one had taken almost twenty minutes but Todd had the hang of it now.

Again and again he knelt between the thighs of the women and thrust the hanger up inside them, through their cervix into the womb, jerking and pulling, tearing and ripping their insides, as he fished around for the fetuses inside of them and tore them out of them piece by piece.

The kitchen floor looked like the floor of a slaughterhouse. It was covered in blood and clumps of flesh and tissue. There were some parts that were clearly arms or legs or heads or torsos, so small that they resembled broken toys but they had all once been alive and would have been born and grown up to pollute the earth with their wastes and drain it of its resources had Todd not done what had to be done.

Todd stood back and looked at all of it, the blood, the traumatized women bleeding on the floor or still strapped to the chairs. Their vaginas looked like raw bleeding meat, torn and lacerated by the hanger. There were still two more women. Todd picked up the knife he'd dropped into the kitchen sink. He was exhausted, too exhausted to use the hanger. The knife would be much quicker. He grabbed the black woman and laid her down on the kitchen table. He was just about to carve her up with the knife when he remembered the scalpels. The cuts would be much cleaner. If he used the scalpel and stitched her up like he'd done Nicolene, she'd probably survive. Todd reached into the bag and grabbed the last roll of tape. He needed to immobilize her if he was going to perform a Caesarian without the woman dying on the table. Unlike Nicolene, she was not doped up on street pharmaceuticals. This woman had nothing to dull the pain.

Todd wrapped the tape around her thighs and legs. When he was certain she could not move, he made the first incision, cutting through her transverse abdominous and the rectus abdominous and pushing the muscles aside revealing the uterus covered by a transparent layer of tissue. He cut through the uterus and dragged the baby out of her belly. The baby was already dead. He pushed the woman off the table and grabbed the last one, a young Puerto Rican girl. He laid her on the kitchen table in the black woman's blood and reached into his bag for another scalpel.

Twenty-One

Todd was completely covered in blood. He peeled his clothes off and walked upstairs. There were babies crying in a room down the hall. He had been too late to stop them from being born and he couldn't imagine himself taking the life of a fully developed child. Instead, Todd stepped into the bathroom mid-way down the hall and into the shower to wash the blood and tissue from his skin.

His mind was clouded by images of Stephanie, his mother sitting on the toilet with a hanger in her vagina pierced through the skull of what would have been his younger brother; Nicolene and the two girls down stairs with their guts laid open, and the big woman whose fetus he'd dragged out of her womb with his bare hands. Todd began to scream. He screamed long and hard and sobbed as if the world had ended. He collapsed into the tub and huddled into a fetal position, still screaming, the shower, now cold, still spraying down on him. When he finally stopped screaming, he heard the front door open and one of the girls run out of the house screaming. Todd leapt up from the shower and ran through the house looking for the old man's room. He needed new clothes. He found some pants and a cardigan, slipped them on, stepped back into his bloody sneakers and sprinted downstairs.

He didn't have his bike. He didn't have a car and the subway was several blocks away. When he stepped outside, Todd saw the large woman he'd bent over the sink banging on the door of a house across the street. Todd began to run. A car raced up the block and Todd ran as hard and as fast as he could. Still, the vehicle caught up with him and slowed down, keeping pace with his stride.

"Todd!"

He turned and was surprised to see his supervisor, Ms. Santiago, sitting behind the wheel of her Saturn hybrid, waving him toward her car. Todd slowed down, panting hard but looking at her suspiciously.

"Elizabeth? Wh—? Wa—? What? What are you doing? What are you doing here?"

She opened her passenger side door.

"Your ex-girlfriend lived. The cops are looking for you everywhere. Get in. I'll take you to the airport." She held up a plane ticket.

Todd walked over to her car.

"Why are you doing this? You know what I've done?"

Elizabeth Santiago smiled, that same bemused expression she'd had when the cops had come to the job to question him. "I'm just throwing a starfish back into the ocean."

Todd got into the car. He sat in the passenger seat looking at her, bewildered and surprised.

"Zero Population?"

"Of course. And I've got another surprise for you."

Twenty-Two

"How soon can I go to the airport? I'm kinda freakin' out just sittin' here."

Todd whispered into the cell phone Elizabeth had given him, nervously looking around the room as if he expected a SWAT team to come crashing through the wall at any moment.

"Your flight doesn't leave until morning. You don't want to just hang around at the airport all night. That might not be safe."

Todd sat on the bed in the dingy airport hotel rocking back and forth and sweating despite the air conditioning. His only comfort was that Elizabeth had booked the room in her name so there would be no trace. But he'd had to show his ID to claim the room and he wasn't sure there wasn't some way to use that to trace him though he figured they'd probably have to call around to every hotel in LA to do it.

He'd fought with the front desk clerk over leaving a credit card for incidentals and finally got the man to agree to use the credit card on file, the one in Elizabeth's name. The man had looked suspicious but didn't look like the type to call the cops. But neither did Todd look like the type to pull the fetus out of a woman with his bare hands and stomp it to death.

"I'm in Los Angeles now. No one is going to be looking for me at the airport here. But I feel like a sitting duck in this motel."

"If anyone checks your flight info they'll see that you flew into LA. That would make the airport the last place you'd want to be. Sorry, Todd but you're going to have to sit tight. There are no other flights tonight anyway."

Elizabeth hadn't had time to get him a fake I.D. so he'd had to use his real name to catch the plane, expecting to get ambushed by airport security or the FBI at every turn. He'd nearly fainted going through the security checkpoint. Elizabeth was right. His name on the plane ticket left a neon trail for anyone with half a brain to follow.

"There has to be a flight somewhere? I'll go anywhere as long as it's out of the country."

"Beggars can't be choosy, Todd. I'm not going to change your destination. Besides, there's a reason that you're going there. You've got more work to do."

"I'm not doing any more abortions."

Todd could almost hear Elizabeth smile through the phone.

"Good night, Todd. Get some sleep. You've got a lot of travelling to do in the morning."

She hung up the phone before Todd could reply. Todd considered calling her back before he put the phone down on the night stand. He stared across the room remembering everything he'd done in the last two days, all the blood, the muffled screams and eyes filled with terror. There was no way he was going to get any sleep tonight.

Todd crawled under the covers fully dressed. He picked up the TV remote and switched on the TV that sat across the room in an entertainment center that looked like an old fashioned armoire. Todd stared at the Shopping Network for what seemed like hours. His mind wasn't registering a thing on the screen. He kept thinking about Stephanie…and Cathy.

The big woman would probably be sitting by Stephanie's bedside comforting her and telling her all about how she was going to make Todd suffer for what he'd done. Stephanie may not have died but she wouldn't exactly be up and walking around either, not after the beating her belly had taken. He only hoped that Cathy would be too worried about Stephanie to leave her bedside. Todd wasn't worried about the police or the FBI. All they could do was arrest him. He didn't want to think about the things Cathy could do to him. He had to get out of here.

Todd had already spent five hours on a plane. Another eight hours waiting around for his next flight would give Cathy a lot of time to track him down. She'd know that he was running and he didn't think she'd be so emotionally distraught over Stephanie that she would let his trail get cold. She'd be right on his ass.

If he didn't get the hell out of there soon he'd be looking down the barrel of Cathy's nine before he could make his connection.

I should have killed her before I left.

Todd looked out the window. It was still dark. He looked back at the TV screen where a B-list celebrity whose name he couldn't remember was trying to sell Teflon cookware endorsed by an A-list chef whose name Todd had never heard of. It seemed like morning would never arrive.

Twenty-Three

Todd didn't know when he'd fallen asleep but he'd almost overslept. He called down to the front desk and asked for a taxi to the airport. Fifteen minutes later he was sitting in the back of a yellow cab pulling into the airport looking for departing flights. "I need the international terminals."

"No problem."

They pulled to a halt in front of the airport and Todd slipped the cabdriver a twenty and then sprinted into the airport. He went to one of the electronic kiosks to print his ticket and then went directly to the security checkpoint. His plane had already started boarding and was scheduled to depart in twenty minutes. If he didn't get there soon he'd miss his flight.

The line was short which meant that the security guards had time to actually do their jobs. A couple of homeland security officers were checking IDs at the front of the line before sending passengers through the metal detectors.

Great. Just what I needed. Todd thought.

Todd checked and then double checked himself for metal objects. He didn't have so much as a set of keys or some loose change. He was still wearing the old man's pants with a pair of flip-flops and a t-shirt he'd bought at the hotel. He had no baggage and he wondered if that would look suspicious. Who left the country without bags?

Maybe I should buy a suitcase? He thought. But there was no time.

He scanned the crowd looking for anyone who looked out of place, anyone who might be giving him too much scrutiny. Everyone looked normal. Just the normal tourists and business men. He was the only one who looked the least bit odd.

He saw a tall woman with a blonde crew-cut and broad shoulders. His heartbeat raced.

Oh shit. Is that Cathy?

He squinted across the crowded airport trying to get a good look at the woman but she was too far away. The woman ducked into the women's bathroom before Todd could get a better look at her. Todd began to perspire again. He started hyperventilating. His vision narrowed until it felt like he was looking at everything through a keyhole. His hearing became muffled like he was underwater. He felt sick and he looked guilty as hell. Todd knew that he had to pull it together. The line was moving quickly and pretty soon he'd be face to face with the security officer. He was almost up to the front of the line.

They're going to think I'm smuggling drugs.

Todd imagined himself being pulled out of line and submitted to a cavity check by brutal men with rubber gloves. He shivered at the thought. He swallowed deeply, took a deep breath and closed his eyes, trying to calm himself. He looked back over his shoulder to see if the woman with the crew-cut was out of the bathroom yet but he didn't see her. Then it was his turn to go through the metal detector.

"ID."

The Homeland Security officer was a middle aged Latino man with pockmarked skin and a thick neck. Todd nervously held out his ID and his plane ticket. The officer looked at the ID and then back up at Todd then back down at the ID. When he looked at Todd the second time Todd was almost certain the man was going to pull him out of line and arrest him.

"Have a nice day, sir."

Todd sighed and forced a smile. He kicked off his shoes, removed his belt and walked through the metal detector just as the woman with the crew-cut left the women's room. She was too far away for Todd to see her clearly but he was almost certain that it was Cathy. Somehow, she had found him. Todd rushed to the terminal. If he was lucky, he would just barely make his flight. Then it wouldn't matter if that was Cathy or not. He'd be long gone. Then he remembered his plane ticket. It was in his own name just like the one that had brought him to Los Angeles. Anyone smart enough to trace him to LA would also be smart enough to find his connecting flight.

Oh well, there's nothing I can do about that now.

His plane was still boarding when Todd arrived at the terminal. He stepped into line behind an elderly black couple and shuffled down the runway sweating and jittering the entire time as if he were going through withdrawals. He shifted nervously from foot to foot and kept looking behind him. Yesterday he had been prepared to die or go to prison but now, with freedom so close, he was petrified that he'd be apprehended or killed before he could get away.

As Todd boarded the airplane he continued to examine the other passengers. He watched as they crammed their bags into the overhead compartments and wriggled and jostled their way into their seats wondering which one of them was really a cop and why it was taking them so long to arrest him. He expected a sky marshal to handcuff him and pull him off the plane at any moment or for Cathy to suddenly burst onto the plane with guns blazing. He didn't relax until the plane's wheels left the tarmac and it began its ascent. He'd been in the sky for less than twenty minutes when exhaustion finally overcame him. Todd leaned his head against the window and stared out at the clouds. Soon he was fast asleep. He didn't awake until the wheels touched down ten hours later and the fasten seatbelt sign went off .

Twenty-Four

Todd exited the plane still reeling from his adventure. He had never expected to still be alive and free. His plan had been to get to as many women as he could before the cops caught up with him and then to kill himself. But he hadn't counted on Ms. Santiago's help. All the years he'd worked with her and he'd never known that they were members of the same environmentalist group. She told him that she'd only figured it out after she'd read a post on the Zero Population message board asking if it was okay to talk a woman into having an abortion and then the very next day Todd had been accused of doing that very thing. Since then she'd been following him. She'd seen what he did to Nicolene.

"I still don't understand why you're helping me though? Talking a woman into having an abortion is one thing but what I've done…" Todd's expression went blank and he'd stared off into the distance. Elizabeth dismissed his concerns with a wave of her hand as if he were merely being childish.

"I've been part of Heimlich's group for five years. I was in on his plan. I was given a different task. They sent me to dairy farms. I've been putting Progesterex in milk vats at some of the biggest dairy farms in the country. Dairy farms that ship products all over the world. I'd been at it for two weeks. I figured that if I put it in the milk, all of those women drinking milk during their pregnancies would find themselves experiencing premature menopause and spontaneous abortions. Heimlich didn't think it was enough. That's why he decided to put it in the water." Todd still couldn't believe it. She'd paid for his plane ticket and drove him to the airport and now here he was, in Sao Paulo, Brazil where no one would be looking for him.

He walked down to baggage claim and a man in a dark suit stood there holding a small sign that said "Hammerstein." Todd walked over to him.

"I'm Todd...Todd Hammerstein."

"Hi, I'm Vitor. Elizabeth sent me. There's a car waiting up front."

Todd followed Vitor to a small economy car that looked more like an oversized golf cart.

"It's electric. Environmentally friendly."

That was the last word he said as they drove through the labyrinthine streets of one of the biggest and most over-crowded cities in the world. They drove for two hours whipping in and out of traffic that made LA look like a quiet country road, darting down narrow streets at 60 miles an hour until they finally reached their destination. Vitor reached behind the seat and handed Todd a new messenger bag.

"This is for you. Elizabeth said you'd know what to do."

Todd took the bag and stepped out of the car. Vitor smiled at him as he looked into the bag, he must have known what was inside. Todd was pretty sure he did too. He looked at the twenty little paper bags stacked inside. He opened one and it was filled with hundreds of tiny blue pills with the letter "P" stamped into them. He smiled and looked up at the sign on the building and the acres of pools filled with water beyond it.

"Departamento de Sao Paulo do Tratamento da Agua"

Even though he had no idea how to speak Portuguese, Todd was pretty sure he knew what it meant just as he knew what was in those pills.

He walked around to the side of the building and scaled the gate, dropping down beside one of the vast pools of water. He opened up a paper bag and began dumping the pills into the water. He opened the next bag and the next one, emptying their contents into the water basins. He was just about to open the next bag when a loud boom echoed in his ears and a burning pain speared through his back and into his chest. He tried to inhale and blood bubbled up in his lungs. Todd turned slowly as black spots danced before his eyes.

The world tilted and shifted out of focus. He didn't need to see straight to recognize the person walking toward him aiming the gun at his head.

"Hello, Cathy."

The next shot knocked Todd off of his feet and into the water. Todd sank to the bottom of the water basin. He knew that he was dying. His lungs were filling with water and he had two bullet holes in his chest. He could see Cathy's face above him contorted in rage, the messenger bag still floating on the surface, the remaining paper bags falling out into the water and all those little pills spilling out of the bags and dissolving.

ABOUT THE AUTHOR

WRATH JAMES WHITE is a former World Class Heavyweight Kickboxer, a professional Kickboxing and Mixed Martial Arts trainer, distance runner, performance artist, and former street brawler, who is now known for creating some of the most disturbing works of fiction in print .

Wrath's two most recent novels are THE RESURRECTIONIST and YACCUB'S CURSE. He is also the author of SUCCULENT PREY, EVERYONE DIES FAMOUS IN A SMALL TOWN, THE BOOK OF A THOUSAND SINS, HIS PAIN and POPULATION ZERO. He is the coauthor of TERATOLOGIST cowritten with the king of extreme horror, Edward Lee, ORGY OF SOULS cowritten with Maurice Broaddus, HERO cowritten with J.F. Gonzalez, and POISONING EROS cowritten with Monica J. O'Rourke.

Wrath lives and works in Austin, Texas with his two daughters, Isis and Nala, his son Sultan and his wife Christie.

deadite
press

"Brain Cheese Buffet" Edward Lee - collecting nine of Lee's most sought after tales of violence and body fluids. Featuring the Stoker nominated "Mr. Torso," the legendary gross-out piece "The Dritiphilist," the notorious "The McCrath Model SS40-C, Series S," and six more stories to test your gag reflex.
"Edward Lee's writing is fast and mean as a chain saw revved to full-tilt boogie."
  - Jack Ketchum

"Bullet Through Your Face" Edward Lee - No writer is more extreme, perverted, or gross than Edward Lee. His world is one of psychopathic redneck rapists, sex addicted demons, and semen stealing aliens. Brace yourself, the king of splatterspunk is guaranteed to shock, offend, and make you laugh until you vomit.
"Lee pulls no punches."
  - Fangoria

"Zombies and Shit" Carlton Mellick III - *Battle Royale* meets *Return of the Living Dead* in this post-apocalyptic action adventure. Twenty people wake to find themselves in a boarded-up building in the middle of the zombie wasteland. They soon realize they have been chosen as contestants on a popular reality show called Zombie Survival. Each contestant is given a backpack of supplies and a unique weapon. Their goal: be the first to make it through the zombie-plagued city to the pick-up zone alive. A campy, trashy, punk rock gore fest.

"Slaughterhouse High" Robert Devereaux - It's prom night in the Demented States of America. A place where schools are built with secret passageways, rebellious teens get zippers installed in their mouths and genitals, and once a year one couple is slaughtered and the bits of their bodies are kept as souvenirs. But something's gone terribly wrong when the secret killer starts claiming a far higher body count than usual . . .
"A major talent!" - Poppy Z. Brite

"The Book of a Thousand Sins" Wrath James White - Welcome to a world of Zombie nymphomaniacs, psychopathic deities, voodoo surgery, and murderous priests. Where mutilation sex clubs are in vogue and torture machines are sex toys. No one makes it out alive – not even God himself.

"If Wrath James White doesn't make you cringe, you must be riding in the wrong end of a hearse."
-Jack Ketchum

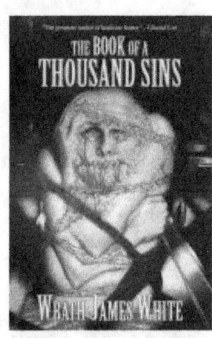

"Squid Pulp Blues" Jordan Krall - In these three bizarro-noir novellas, the reader is thrown into a world of murderers, drugs made from squid parts, deformed gun-toting veterans, and a mischievous apocalyptic donkey.

". . . with SQUID PULP BLUES, [Krall] created a wholly unique terrascape of Ibsen-like naturalism and morbidity; an extravaganza of white-trash urban/noir horror."
- Edward Lee

"Apeshit" Carlton Mellick III - Friday the 13th meets Visitor Q. Six hipster teens go to a cabin in the woods inhabited by a deformed killer. An incredibly fucked-up parody of B-horror movies with a bizarro slant

"The new gold standard in unstoppable fetus-fucking killfreakomania . . . Genuine all-meat hardcore horror meets unadulterated Bizarro brainwarp strangeness. The results are beyond jaw-dropping, and fill me with pure, unforgivable joy." - John Skipp

"Super Fetus" Adam Pepper - Try to abort this fetus and he'll kick your ass!

"The story of a self-aware fetus whose morally bankrupt mother is desperately trying to abort him. This darkly humorous novella will surely appall and upset a sizable percentage of people who read it . . . In-your-face, allegorical social commentary."
- BarnesandNoble.com

THE VERY BEST IN CULT HORROR

deadite
Press

"Rock and Roll Reform School Zombies" Bryan Smith - Sex, Death, and Heavy Metal! The Southern Illinois Music Reeducation Center specializes in "de-metaling" – a treatment to cure teens of their metal loving, devil worshiping ways. A program that subjects its prisoners to sexual abuse, torture, and brain-washing. But tonight things get much worse. Tonight the flesh-eating zombies come . . . *Rock and Roll Reform School Zombies* is Bryan Smith's tribute to "Return of the Living Dead" and "The Decline of Western Civilization Part 2: the Metal Years."

"Necro Sex Machine" Andre Duza - America post apocalypse...a toxic wasteland populated by blood-thristy scavengers, mutated animals, and roving bands of organized militias wing for control of civilized society's leftovers. Housed in small settlements that pepper the wasteland, the survivors of the third world war struggle to rebuild amidst the scourge of sickness and disease and the constant threat of attack from the horrors that roam beyond their borders. But something much worse has risen from the toxic fog.

"Piecemeal June" Jordan Krall - Kevin lives in a small apartment above a porn shop with his tarot-reading cat, Mithra.She brings him things from outside and one day-brings him an rubber-latex ankle... Later an eyeball, then a foot. After more latex body parts are brought upstairs, Kevin glues them together to form a piecemeal sex doll. But once the last piece is glued into place, the sex doll comes to life. She says her name is June. She comes from another world and is on the run from an evil pornographer and three crab-human hybrid assassins.

"The Vegan Revolution . . . with Zombies" David Agranoff - Thanks to a new miracle drug the cute little pig no longer feels a thing as she is led to the slaughter. The only problem? Once the drug enters the food supply anyone who eats it is infected. From fast food burgers to free-range organic eggs, eating animal products turns people into shambling brain-dead zombies – not even vegetarians are safe!
"A perfect blend of horror, humor and animal activism."
    - Gina Ranalli

"Dead Bitch Army" Andre Duza - Step into a world filled with racist teenagers, masked assassins, cannibals, a telekinetic hitman, 100 warped Uncle Sams, automobiles with razor-sharp teeth, living graffiti, cartoons that walk and talk, a steroid-addicted pro-athlete, an angry black chic, a washed-up Barbara Walters clone, the threat of a war to end all wars, and a pissed-off zombie bitch out for revenge.

"Fistful of Feet" Jordan Krall - A bizarro tribute to Spaghetti westerns, H.P. Lovecraft, and foot fetish enthusiasts. Screwhorse, Nevada is legendary for its violent and unusual pleasures, but when a mysterious gunslinger drags a wooden donkey into the desert town, the stage is set for a bloodbath unlike anything the west has ever seen. Featuring Cthulhu-worshipping Indians, a woman with four feet, a Giallo-esque serial killer, Syphilis-ridden mutants, ass juice, burping pistols, sexually transmitted tattoos, and a house devoted to the freakiest fetishes, Jordan Krall's *Fistful of Feet* is the weirdest western ever written.

"Trolley No. 1852" Edward Lee - In 1934, horror writer H.P. Lovecraft is invited to write a story for a subversive underground magazine, all on the condition that a pseudonym will be used. The pay is lofty, and God knows, Lovecraft needs the money. There's just one catch. It has to be a pornographic story . . . The 1852 Club is a bordello unlike any other. Its women are the most beautiful and they will do anything. But there is something else going on at this sex club. In the back rooms monsters are performing vile acts on each other and doors to other dimensions are opening . . .

"Super Fetus" Adam Pepper - Try to abort this fetus and he'll kick your ass!
"The story of a self-aware fetus whose morally bankrupt mother is desperately trying to abort him. This darkly humorous novella will surely appall and upset a sizable percentage of people who read it . . . In-your-face, allegorical social commentary."
- BarnesandNoble.com

AVAILABLE FROM AMAZON.COM